About the author

L.K. Lemay is passionate about writing. She has written several novels, screenplays and children's books, including *The Joy of Growing Old Disgracefully*; a children's novel and screenplay, *Bin There*; three children's picture books, *Furry Godmother*, *Aqua Dragon* and *Bear on the Run*.

Her main aim is to entertain and bring a feel-good factor to all those who enjoy her work.

DYING TO DO IT

L. K. Lemay

DYING TO DO IT

Vanguard Press

A CIP catalogue record for this title is
available from the British Library.

ISBN 978 1 80016 183 2

*Vanguard Press is an imprint of
Pegasus Elliot MacKenzie Publishers Ltd.*
www.pegasuspublishers.com

First Published in 2021

**Vanguard Press
Sheraton House Castle Park
Cambridge England**

Printed & Bound in Great Britain

Dedication

To my beautiful family for their listening and feedback.

Acknowledgements

To Margaret H for your continued support.

FINDING OUT
TUESDAY 2ND MAY
3.40 p.m.

No one likes visiting the doctors, do they?

At our surgery, the experience is made even more uncomfortable because of the daft systems and difficult staff.

I've had a letter, calling me in. I've tried to ignore it, but my common sense has overtaken my reticence. I am sure I've already had some results from the 'Well Woman' check-up, but I feel I should go anyway.

I have just driven to the surgery for my 3.40 p.m. appointment. You can feel the uneasy atmosphere, immediately you enter the building. I hate bullying and I hate myself for ignoring the receptionist's rudeness, but I need to get back to work.

Maybe it doesn't bother poor Mrs Walters as much as it bothers me? As if. She is squirming because of her lack of technical knowledge. There seems to be a void developing between those who are tech savvy and those who just haven't kept up to date, because they thought they didn't need to. Mrs Walters has no idea how to check in electronically on the new screen. Neither do I, but I'm not in the firing line because they already have a victim as I arrive. This gives me time to watch the instructions, sarcastically delivered by Amy, the surly receptionist's dummy. I manage to copy the system and sign in before they can turn their attention back to me.

An old couple, sensing the growing tension, decide they have a bus to catch and beat a hasty retreat.

I appease my conscience by chatting to Mrs Walters, out of sight, but obviously not out of ear-shot, to help her to keep buoyant. This does not go down well with the receptionist 'prison guards.'

I hate myself for avoiding eye contact, but Mrs Walters warns me not to react, as the Gestapo would be only too keen to call for security, whoever they are? Apparently, they threatened her with the very same last week. This doesn't surprise me. To my left I see Amy scuttle off down the corridor and return a few minutes later. She looks too pleased with herself.

I am reading the notice on the wall, complaining about all the missed appointments. I am considering writing a reply, explaining that it's so difficult to get an appointment, by the time they see you, you've either sorted yourself out or died. I'm feeling pleased with myself, even though I've done nothing about the notice, until they return for another go.

Sandra waves Mrs Walters across to the desk, like Barbara Woodhouse teaching a dog to herd sheep. A form is pushed at Mrs W. whilst Sandra explains to her in short, sharp phrases how to sign her name and add the date. Really?

'Just here, 02, 05, 18, sign means your name.' Every time the young girl speaks, she raises her eyebrows to Ms Amy Grice, the other inquisitor receptionist.

I've had enough. I can see Mrs Walters about to exit the building and she obviously needs to sort out her medical problem, or she wouldn't be here, putting up with this.

I stare at them, now I've decided to make very strong eye contact. This delights them, somehow. They pseudo sweetly direct me down the corridor. 'Doctor Carten will see you now.'

I have to leave Mrs W. to her own devices.

The young receptionist takes further delight in informing me that the regular doctor is unavailable and that Dr Carten has taken his place. I wonder if Dr Carten is handsome and whether this is the reason for her amusement? I scoot past the reception and deliver a nonchalant 'OK,' as they shout directions down the corridor at me. I can feel their eyes in my back.

***

The new locum looks nervous when I enter the surgery. He isn't that good looking, in my opinion. I wait to be invited to sit, but then realise he is in his own little world, so lower myself strategically into the chair. I wait.

Dr Carten looks about ten, well, maybe sixteen. He is clearly uneasy, but I ignore this. Who wouldn't be, working in this environment?

He asks me if, 'I know why I am here?'

I explain that they have called me in and that I'd already had some results back from the Well Woman clinic, much earlier and that it might be something more to do with the blood tests? Then I wait some more.

I hear the next part about, 'Not really, difficult news.'

I become increasingly nervous when he asks if I have anyone with me.

At 'brain tumour' my pulse starts beating so fast that it becomes one long thread of pressure. He does not know how long I have left. I can see his mouth moving but the pounding is so loud in my ears that I cannot assimilate the words. I leave the room on my feet, but immediately in the corridor, I start to reel and lose consciousness.

I manage to get into a room, which I think is a toilet and get the projectile vomit into a sink. After that I black out and slide down to the floor.

***

When I come around, I can see through a small frosted window that it is still light outside, but I can't hear anyone in the building. I shiver. I think about calling for help but then try to find my mobile in my bag instead.

Who to call? I think to myself. I'll have to tell Daisy and Luke if I ask them for help. Who do I know well enough to ring and say, 'Help, I'm locked in a broom cupboard?' Dougie would find it so hilarious, he'd probably post me looking wretched on Facebook, just for the laugh.

It is seven o'clock. The mop bucket at the side of me stinks. I scramble to my feet and try the door, it is stuck. I continue to tug, it moves a little. I try to compose myself, wiping my mouth and running the tap to remove the remains of my stomach from the sink. I am pleased I had a light lunch.

After a concerted effort, the door gives way and I am able to enter the corridor and main building. I am relieved not to be locked in. There are no lights on and everything is closed down. I start to try the phone, then think better of it. Pressing a switch brings the surveillance cameras to life. I can see the front door, the reception area and what looks like a doctor's surgery. I turn to see the emergency exit and I almost run, when an inner voice makes me act more strategically. I put a towel around my head and lever the door open with the long handle. Outside I push it shut behind me.

The smell of fresh air, out in the surgery grounds is intoxicating. I walk briskly down the pathway until I reach my car. I drop to the ground at the side of the car and check for any cameras; before sliding into the driving seat, starting the car and leaving the street.

After driving for several minutes, I pull the car into the side of a quiet road. I can smell the aroma of fish and chips and the realisation that I am hungry and therefore functioning correctly makes me cry.

It could also be the song, *Change* by The Sugarbabes, which starts to play on the radio.

I start to talk to myself.

Diet says no, mind says yes. Then I laugh as I leave my car.

***

It has taken fifteen awkward minutes to queue for my fish supper, but the smell alone makes the effort, worth it.

Driving away from the street and into the start of the countryside, I see a lay-by and pull in. The food is well received and I eat until I am full. The aroma of cheap vinegar has the ability to numb my memory as I become lost in the joy of the food. I can, however, only eat half of the meal.

I am about to leave the car to approach the waste bin with my leftovers, when a large blue BMW whisks past me and pulls up, just past the bin.

A man in jeans, a smart shirt and loafers, jumps out of the driver's side and takes a large cardboard box from his boot, placing it on the roadside and immediately driving off.

I shout after him, 'You've left your box,' even though I realise he knows this.

Not my problem, I think to myself and shrug. As I am turning away, the box moves and there is a short squeal. I approach the box. *BOOM,* I declare, then ask myself, *Why are you opening suspect packages?*

Then worryingly I reply:

Well at least it would be a quick and a relatively painless way to go. Not yet though. I need to check the kids are OK.

Peering into the box makes me cover my mouth with both hands.

You hear about people abandoning pets, but when you see it first hand, it still shocks.

There are three of the cutest puppies in the box, staring with pleading eyes for some help.

'The rotten bugger,' I exclaim to no one in particular.

I'm already in shut-down mode and turn quickly on my heel and head back to my car. Driving off is the most gut-wrenching experience. I wonder how I'm going to do it to my children? Just the word 'leave' overwhelms me and I pull out dangerously through streaming tears.

I'm sorry mates, but I'm no use to you. I won't be here long enough.

Five minutes down the road, my composure returns and with it, my conscience.

I turn the car around and head back. The box is still there, but open. I quickly run to it. Two of the puppies are still inside. There is a squeal from the field next to the road. I run towards it. There is a row of crows starting to circle the young dog. They run at it and peck, drawing blood. The pup is terrified. Above the posse is a large chestnut coloured bird of prey, watching from a tree. The huge bird swoops and lifts the pup into the air. He cries out in fear. Another similar bird of prey appears.

This is more than I can stand. I run in and collect the dazed puppy as it drops to the ground, some way away. Carrying him back across the field of wheat stubble, I glare at the crows, who sit insolently watching the events. Returning the pup to the box with his siblings, I place this on the passenger seat of the car and return to the field.

I search the area for sticks and missiles, but only manage to pull up large sods of muddy soil from the harvested wheat field. This is enough to arm me against the attackers. I go in like a cornered beast, screaming and whooping, a lone lioness, defending her cubs, from a pack of jackals, until the birds have shown me some respect and moved away.

I share my satisfaction with the puppies. 'How very therapeutic!' I offer.

The emotion starts me off crying again, but the puppies join in so I manage to contain myself as we drive home, because their cries are far more highly pitched and empathic.

HOME
TUESDAY 2ND MAY
8.50 p.m.

After bandaging the puppy's leg, I put some water and ham in their box. I really have no idea what they eat.

I start searching through cupboards and drawers for my will. The last thing I want to do is leave my money to Dougie. Maybe a little something, but I don't trust him to be fair.

I find a kitchen knife and hold it up. A pup's head appears as it tries to scramble out of the box. I explain the knife is not for them. As though they understand.

'Let's hope it doesn't come to this. I'm vegetarian. It will never work.'

I sit on the sofa.

***

The next thing I know is that I've fallen asleep.

I wake feeling very wet and realise the pups have escaped their box and are lying next to me. Ah, I realise they are not yet toilet trained. They whine and twist themselves over my body. This presses the cold damp moisture against my skin, making me jump to my feet.

A glance in the box informs me they haven't touched the ham pieces.

'Do you miss your mum? Let's try this.'

I sing to them as I pour some milk in a saucer. The pups cry even more.

I plead with them. 'Come on guys, please be quiet?'

Again, I return them to their box and add some newspaper, for comfort. I change my clothes from a basket of clean washing on the table. The discarded ones are thrown in a heap in the corner. Settling down on the sofa, I quickly drift back into sleep. Images of the ill-mannered doctors' receptionists, Acid Amy and Smirking Sarah, flash in and out of my mind, as I toss and turn.

***

I wake again to the now familiar feeling of dog urine dripping down my leg.

'Oh my, what have I done?'

Light is streaming in through the window and the dawn is shining through. The resident blackbird is clicking an alarmed warning. There must be a cat on the prowl. Once she has settled, this gives way to a melody of tranquil birdsong. Savouring every moment of the day is a skill I am keen to learn. Now I feel Edward Thomas's poetry. I want to share it with the puppies.

'Wow look at this amazing new day. Let's do happy things?'

The dogs are asleep.

Typical.

I walk to the window, picking up my hairbrush on the way. The light has a luminous quality as the moon bows in acquiescence to the sun's growing glory.

I return to a mirror on the cabinet, sink into the chair and stare into my own eyes. I brush my beautiful hair gently, as tears stream down my face.

***

I wake hours later in the armchair by the mirror because the dogs are chasing around the room, which is now covered in torn paper and dog excrement. I don't have time to clean up, because I want to get to the vet's as early as possible.

THE VET'S
WEDNESDAY 3RD MAY
8.30 a.m.

I am relieved to find this vet practice on the internet and they agree to see us immediately. This does not make me suspicious. The girl on the desk assumes I am trying to pass the puppies off, even though I'm not. They must get a lot of this sort of thing. On being asked what the injured pup's name is, I draw a blank. From somewhere in my psyche, I conjure up, 'Foxy.'

We all sit, the pups in a large laundry basket, inside a larger open-topped bag. We watch as a Golden Labrador is dragged into the surgery by an old, tall, grey-looking man. The dog literally slides on her bottom across the room, as she resists the direction of the pulling. The man hands the lead to the receptionist and she passes him a clipboard for him to sign.

"If you're sure?' she checks.

The man nods dispassionately and the dog is taken into another nearby room. She looks so sad.

We are called into the vet's room.

'Could Foxy go into Mr Buckland's surgery, please?'

She repeats the request, this time staring at me.

I don't realise at first because I don't recognise Foxy's name, until the receptionist makes it obvious. I laugh, partly from embarrassment, then I struggle down the corridor with the subdued pups.

The surgery is clean and bright. The vet seems approachable.

'Foxy was attacked by a horde of crows,' I begin. 'If that is the collective noun?'

Apparently, it's also a 'murder', I'm informed by the vet.

How apt I think. He goes on to call Foxy a bitch, which I begin to take exception to, then realise it is the technical term for a female dog.

Umm, got that bit wrong then. I ask the vet to tell me the sex of the other two dogs. They are male. Foxy then has her leg cleaned and is given an injection. I start to relax.

'I know you might tell me to mind my own business, but is that lovely Labrador ill? She looks really well,' I ask.

The vet tells me that this is the worse part of his job, putting healthy animals down and that the owner will not even let them take the dog to the RSPCA.

Whilst I am ready to take the matter further (now that I have taken on the role of St Francis of Assisi), the vet stings me with a bill for £90.

I gather the dogs and scarper before he charges me for his time with the other two pups.

As we walk down the corridor, we pass the Labrador, still tied to a bar on the wall.

Her eyes speak to me as I try to pass. Once again, my conscience knows no reserve. To myself I whisper, 'Sod it.'

I put the bag of pups on the floor and loosen the Labradors lead. She wriggles free and sets off through the door and out of the building.

Carrying the bag of puppies, I shout, as I swiftly negotiate past the busy reception area, 'I'll be back… to pay.'

THE CHASE
WEDNESDAY 3rd MAY
9.50 a.m.

As we leave the vet's building, a mobility scooter is parked right across the entrance. A middle-aged woman is loading groceries into the pannier on the back. All I can see is her backside. After a sudden lurch forward, I manage not to bump into her. I am at least half a mile from my car. I can see the Labrador heading at speed down the street. I imagine her running back to her nasty owner. Instinct kicks in again. Dropping the pups into the front basket of the scooter, I pack the laundry bag around them and slide surreptitiously onboard. The motor is running and the keys are in the ignition. From the mirror on the handlebars, I can see the mobility scooter's owner, her face getting smaller and yet redder, as she realises what is happening. She looks shocked. She looks shocked, as fortuitously for us, she stumbles backwards. We set off precariously, wobbling from side to side. When she has regained composure, the woman starts shouting 'Thief,' whilst chasing us down the street, her face following behind us, becoming increasingly distorted and enraged. The pups are jostling about and bumping from side to side. I try to pack the bag around them to wedge them in.

I can hear George Ezra's, 'It don't matter now,' playing as we pass the shops. There is no sign of the adult dog.

I shout behind me, 'Don't worry, I'll explain later, I'll be as quick as I can.'

The puppies yap for a while. Luckily, we spot the Labrador as she crosses the end of a street and we pick up the scent again. Several voices can now be heard behind us.

A car draws alongside us. The children in the back of the car are shouting and waving. The pups become even more excited. A man is hanging out of the passenger door and starts videoing us, as the driver sustains a level speed at our side. I realise my driving position resembles the crazy frog, but this is necessary in the circumstances... and it reduces the air resistance.

I manage to scowl at the amateur paparazzi as I sharply exit down a narrow alley, still pursuing the Labrador.

After several minutes and a journey over cobbles (which could keep a chiropractor in work for decades), the dog enters the grounds of a large house. As I slow down, one of the puppies jumps out of the basket like a parachute pilot and joins the Labrador. I manoeuvre into the impressive entrance drive. I realise my mistake when I see the shadow of a man behind the frosted door glass. Looking for the reverse switch, I intend to depart, however the motor is thoroughly drained and the mobility scooter, refuses to move. Left with no other choice I dart behind a hedge, with the bag and remaining two pups.

The image behind the door glass reveals himself. My, is this worth waiting for! Fit but not muscle bound. Classic in face but still with a quirkiness that, had I the time and the assets to match his beauty, I would have enjoyed exploring.

In short, he is well out of my league. Analysis over, I am now panicking. I suddenly feel ridiculous. How to naturally appear from behind a bush, without losing my credibility? I stand up. I have no other choice. Honey and Foxy are heading towards us and he is following.

'Hello,' I say, trying not to sound too lame.

He replies, 'Good morning.' I am shocked by his politeness, maybe because I'd forgotten men could behave in such a way.

'You certainly seem to have made an impression,' he observes, as all four dogs are now free and chaotically caught up in the excitement of the moment.

'Likewise, she's lovely', I sycophantically reply, whilst stroking Honey. A woman has to make an effort.

'You've got your hands full,' he comments.

I make a concerted effort not to tilt my head to one side, as if to show I am hanging on his every word.

I fail. 'Yes, haven't I?' I whisper agreeably. 'Is she your dog?'

'Yes, my bosom buddy. I've been going out of my mind worrying. She's never run off before. Why do you ask?'

I'm too busy staring into his eyes and realise I need to keep the conversation going, to make this possible, when I can hear shouting in the distance. Grabbing the puppies, I bundle them into the bag. Foxy is making an effort to remain with Honey, so with one last undignified lurch forward, I sweep her up and into my coat. With a crafty look along the street, I set off.

'She just seemed to know her way home so well,' I offer.

'Where from?' he asks.

'I can't tell you now, sorry, I have to go... the vet's on Silver Street,' I shout as quietly as I can. I'm not sure if he's heard me.

I can just hear him as I turn the corner of the street, shout, 'I'm Callum by the way... hang on.'

RIGHT PLACE, RIGHT TIME
WEDNESDAY 3RD MAY
10.40 a.m.

We are running awkwardly along the street. A bus passes us, then stops a little way away from the bus stop.

One person boards the bus, but the driver waits, mainly because I'm doing my wild arm-waving dance as I awkwardly run with the bag of pups and Foxy captured in my coat.

I step up, half expecting the bus to pull away. The driver is staring at my chest, which is moving.

The pups in the bag growl. I touch my mouth with my hand to simulate a burp.

'Oh, excuse me,' I offer.

He isn't buying it and looks at the bag, but takes my two pounds anyway. I hasten to the back seat of the bus. Behind me, through the window, I can see a crowd gathering. They are watching the bus. I make a little inward prayer that the bus moves forward quickly and it does.

Ten minutes later, we are well out of reach and travelling along nicely.

From the corner of my eye, I can see a man walking along the street. He looks a lot like Dougie. I swing around to get a better look. It is Dougie. I'd know that blond mop anywhere. He is arm in arm with a young woman. Another bus pulls behind us and blocks the view.

In my head I am running through the reasons he would legitimately be with another woman, when I realise, we are now entering the bus station. I rush to the front and wedge myself into the queue, alighting quickly and exiting through the door to the supermarket. Once out, I keep my head down and keep walking.

SPYING
WEDNESDAY 3RD MAY
7.30 p.m.

I decide to approach Dougie head on. I'm at his house, it's early evening and his car isn't here. If we are no longer an item, I'd rather know.

Brilliant! Not. That's his mother leaving and I'm sure she's seen me.

George Ezra's, 'It don't matter now', is playing on the radio. I turn it down as I drive towards her. I lower the car window.

'Good evening, Clara,' I offer in good nature.

Immediately she is in vulture mode.

'He's not in, you're wasting your time spying. Is this the only way you can catch him?'

She does nothing to conceal her self-satisfied smirk. 'Maybe you should be more attentive?' she states, rather than offers, as advice.

I think about replying to the rhetorical question and opening the debate about her impact on her son's evolution to manhood... or thereabouts. However, I decide to go in for a counterattack of my own, which I have been saving up my sleeve for a considerable length of time.

'Thank you for your relationship advice.'

I can see my sweetness momentarily disarms her and this encourages me. She does not let up though and prefers to take my change of subject as weakness.

'You should think less about yourself and your career and more about taking care of my son.'

I pause as I think about what her son should be doing in the relationship, which he isn't. Like kindness, integrity and grace.

She takes the pause as acceptance that I agree and is surprised when I reply, 'It's a shame you can't use your own advice to stop your husband straying.'

I turn away so as not to laugh at the look of shock on her face.

Clara replies emphatically in a deeper tone, 'Cyril has never strayed!'

I am more than happy to supply the detail. 'Ask your so-called best friend, Lucy, what happened after you passed out from drink, at Dougie boy's thirtieth party. Lucy's been sniffing round Cyril ever since. Everyone knows. If you took your head out your own backside for one minute, you'd recognise how it really is. Good day.'

I immediately drive away, so she has no time to retort. I need not have worried, as I look in my rear-view mirror, her mouth is still open in shock.

'It Don't Matter Now' creeps into my head.

Looking in the back seat, I can see even the puppies look satisfied. I praise them for their compliance and good behaviour.

'This is it now, guys, putting the world right before I run out of time. Aren't you good puppies?'

Was that a smile? No, now I am losing it.

LOVED ONES
THURSDAY 4TH MAY
6.00 p.m.

I'm waiting for my daughter Daisy outside her offices. I can see she has spotted my car and is making her way over. She looks tired, which isn't good for an twenty-two-year-old and I feel guilty that she has to work.

She greets me with a, 'Hi Mum,' and a hug.

'I can see you're going out with your friends,' I offer, so as not to deter her from her plans.

'No, I don't want to go. Can you give me a lift home? I'm shattered,' she replies.

As we drive along, we chat. 'Are you doing too much?' I enquire.

'It's just constant pressure and sometimes a sleep is the best remedy,' Daisy comments.

'You *did* listen to what I said.' I beam, proud to be her mum. Neither Daisy nor Luke, were close to their father, when he left and didn't come back one night, eight years ago. He had always worked away and had engaged very little in their lives, as they grew up.

I smile because I believe she will be able to look after herself and her younger brother when I'm gone. I hope it's the right decision not to tell her about my issues now. She seems too tired and pre-occupied. I need to be organised to make the process as easy as possible for them both. I think about introducing her to the puppies, whom I have left at the house.

Daisy notices I have gone off into my own world.

'Are you OK?' she asks, as I drop her at her friend's flat.

'I'm fine, darling. Sleep tight. Love you.' I want to hold her to me and not let her go, but I smile instead.

'Love you too,' she says and waves as she lets herself into the front door.

I force a smile long enough for her to be out of sight, then I sob.

Change by the Sugarbabes, flows onto the radio.

PLANNING
THURSDAY 4TH MAY
7.20 p.m.

I am feeling a need to be ready for all eventualities. I don't want to suffer if the pain gets too bad and I'm aware that my capacity to think effectively may well become diminished.

Having watched *Thelma and Louise* with the pups, I've decided not to drive off a cliff. Even though it is a better option than throwing myself under a moving vehicle. Trains have drivers and they would have to carry the repercussions of guilt afterwards… maybe? Depending on who they are, I suppose. My mother used to tell me I thought too deeply into problems. It's who I am.

I tell the pups that, 'I'd rather leave the speed machine to the kids.' It has taken me years to iron out all the idiosyncrasies of the car and to pay for it. I don't like wasting money. However, it does remain on the agenda of escape routes, as it is also fast, should I get into any more trouble and need a quick getaway.

However, to more pressing matters, I still haven't found my will. I cajole the pups into the hallway and block their escape route with a stairgate, before making myself a microwave meal.

The pups are still whining. I try to eat the macaroni cheese with them staring at me. Even at the perfect ambient temperature, the food has no appeal to me. I give it to the pups, who fight over it. 'Success at last,' I tell them. I sound positive but can't seem to stop my eyes welling up with tears.

I decide to ring Douglas. I sort of know he will be his usual charming self.

I've not spoken to him in days and I get a blunt, 'What?'

Followed by, 'Why are you ringing me?'

When I explain I want to speak to him, I get further abuse.

'That's what phones are for.'

'Not over the phone,' I explain. He is unwilling to comply with even this straightforward request and instead directs me to talk to Daisy, who apparently is unhappy. I am immediately uneasy. How does he know this? The thought of her confiding in him sends a shiver up my spine. When he explains they are friends on Facebook, I decide to end the call abruptly so he cannot upset me further.

I bet you are, I say to myself.

The doorbell rings. I check my watch to see how long after the phone call it is and expect Dougie to be standing at the door. To my shock and I confess, delight, it is Callum with Honey.

I immediately think there is something wrong.

'No', he explains. 'I just wanted to thank you for saving Honey, my Labrador. I'm Callum, by the way.'

I feel my face blush, because I heard his name the first time we met, it has swirled sweetly around my subconscious ever since; but it reminds me of my frenetic retreat from his driveway.

'I went to the vet's and they told me they'd had instructions to put Honey down.'

'Who would do such a thing?' I ask. He explains it was his stepfather. I offer a description of, 'old, tall, grey-looking man?'

'Beautifully described.' He laughs. 'It's a long story.'

There is a short and uncomfortable silence.

'I'd invite you in but...' I have raging thoughts about him killing me by strangulation. I step away from the door and welcome him inside. I am ashamed to confess it would be one of my preferred options of euthanasia, if that were required... OK, I'm being facetious. I am relieved that the room is relatively tidy for a puppy sitter's pad.

The puppies go wild when they see Honey. They have to be satisfied with a group hug in the hallway though, because they are still too young to be let out in the garden.

I have been reading up on puppy care on the internet... because I haven't been back to the vet's yet. I leave Callum in the living room whilst I hastily make him a drink. I return and try to ignore how gorgeous he is. We sit on opposite chairs.

He explains, 'So to summarise, my mum has just died. My Stepfather, is trying to fake his death to get *his* life insurance money, because my mother hasn't left him any of hers. (I don't think he was very forthcoming with his contribution to the bills, allegedly).

'He wants me to hide him in the family home, because he thinks I owe him. That's my view of what's happening, anyway. Bizarre as it sounds.'

'I take it she didn't? Leave him any money?' I ask, then wish I hadn't been so forward.

'Not a penny. She may have had her reasons. He keeps appearing at my windows to spook me into agreeing with his absurd plot. I haven't, so he's kept on threatening to kill the dog. I never thought he'd go through with it, though.'

'He didn't have the nerve to do it himself though, did he? Maybe he's not as hard as he thinks he is?'

I offer, hoping this will give Callum comfort.

He points out the obvious. 'Hard enough to try to kill her, though. I was so grateful to you for saving her. I went to the vet's and they gave me your address.'

The thought that they've given out my details for revenge, because I ran off without paying, skips fleetingly across my mind.

I smile and say to Callum, 'Ummm, I'm pleased, but it's a bit naughty of them.'

He replies with a grin, 'Well actually it was Cheryl on the desk. I went to school with her.'

It all falls into place. I'd give him anything. My head starts to tilt agreeably to one side. I sit up and correct myself.

I pay homage to the fact that he is, sizzling hot. 'I bet you can get anything you want, if you put your mind to it?'

It is an objective viewpoint and tinged with my own regret, that I will not be around much longer and should not get too involved. I am reflecting that this is probably to my advantage, because I can then lock down my libido. Then he hits me with a bombshell.

'I didn't give it to the police though,' he nonchalantly adds.

'What do you mean?' I retort, far too quickly, so as to give my fear away.

'They wanted to know why the missing mobility scooter was in my driveway. It's all over the local news,' he explains.

'No!' I utter deeply, then stand.

'Yes. I think the headlines were something like, *Severely disabled victim had her only means of transport stolen from under her nose, by an unscrupulous fraudster.*'

'Wait a minute, she chased me for three streets. She'd have given Usain Bolt a run for his money. Disabled my ar… backside.'

There is a knock at the door.

In my defence, anyone would have panicked in these circumstances.

'What if they followed you here?' I whisper.

''The police? Why would they?' he replies.

I look through the spy hole in my door.

Trying not to give away my unrest, I explain, 'Even worse, It's my fella. He's going to think the wrong thing when he sees you. I've got enough shocking news to tell him. How would you feel about hiding upstairs?'

Callum kindly agrees. 'Wrong, but if it makes you happy.'

I show him to the stairs and he climbs over the puppies,

I let Douglas in.

In true spoilt-brat style, he goes straight for the jugular. 'Good God it stinks in here.'

I take the higher moral ground. 'Don't blaspheme. It's dog excrement.' From the puzzled look on his face, I feel I should have said shit, he'd get that. This gives me a certain sense of satisfaction. I am still smiling as I explain.

'I'm looking after three puppies until I can find them a new home.'

'Oh, Mother Theresa,' he quips. I am amazed he hasn't sworn. I can also tell, he knows I am buoyant, for some reason and this is annoying him.

'What do you want?' I ask.

'Why were you at mine?' he wants to know.

I explain as sarcastically as I can, 'I'm... your girlfriend.'

'Well, stop calling me here for nothing.'

Rather than this squashing my positive mood, I seize the opportunity to get rid of him.

'What? OK. Feel free to go then.'

He senses my urgency. 'I'll go when I'm ready.'

My eyebrows raise involuntarily and a determined steel flows through my blood. I make a mental note to myself to continue this assertive stance. I point to the front of the house.

Douglas leaves via the front door. I am impressed how effective I am.

After the door has banged shut, Callum appears from upstairs.

'I'm sorry,' I offer

Callum seems to want to become involved. I find this sexy, but quash the vibe.

'Look, I can sort of sense something is wrong. Can I help? Maybe give the Laddo a personality transplant?' he suggests.

I am polite but then disintegrate into mischief. 'Thank you for the offer, that's so kind... but it would be a waste of a good brain.'

I continue, 'I don't know where I am at the moment.'

'What about I babysit the puppies for a while? Extra guard dogs for when Stephan, the stepfather, comes around?

A light bulb goes on in my head. I know I have limited time and diminishing resources. The pups would be safe with him at least for now. I know the pups will be delighted. I accept graciously.

'That would enable me to get on top of my bucket list. Are you sure? You don't happen to know what to feed them on, do you?'

FACING THE KRAKEN
FRIDAY 5TH MAY
5.55 p.m.

I decide to visit Dougie, to tell him my news. He lets me in after several minutes wait. Through the window I can see he is lying on the sofa with his bare ugly feet in the air. He is watching the television, ignoring the doorbell.

When he eventually lets me in, I follow him through to the kitchen. He now has shoes on. He starts to hunt for food in the fridge.

'I need to go out and get some food. Can we do this another day?' he asks.

I am determined not to show my frustration and so answer sweetly,

'Yes, I didn't think you'd be in anyway.'

Not one to miss a put down, he retorts, 'What did you come for then?'

I am desperately searching for a response but only manage, 'You know… I took a chance. Thank goodness he isn't the father of my children,' I muse. Then my mind returns to the present and I realise, he is trying to get rid of me.'

We've been together for three years now, he has never done this before. He was actually very well behaved in the first year… wasn't he? I question myself. Thank goodness he isn't the father to my children. Maybe in response to me practically throwing him out of mine, maybe because someone else is scheduled in to visit him.

Dougie walks casually through to the living room and returns to his supine position on the sofa. There are no seats left for me. He turns on the TV by using the remote control and stares at the screen. He increases the volume.

Awkward. I walk through to the kitchen.

He shouts an order for me to return. 'Come here.'

This is too much for me and I alleviate the stress by gesturing V signs angrily from the kitchen, before shouting back sweetly as I leave, 'Look after yourself then.'

I am out of the front door and hear no reply.

I get in my car and drive down the road. Immediately out of sight of his house, I pull into a parking place and walk back towards Dougie's house, crossing over his neighbours' open-plan gardens, so I can keep close to the house edges. I find Dougie's front door slightly ajar, as I have left it.

I can see him through the window and hear him through the door. Dougie is flicking through Tinder profiles on the screen, talking to himself.

'Had her… had her…'

He picks up his phone and I stand motionless as I feel my mobile in my pocket. It does not ring.

Instead, Dougie starts to talk to someone else.

'Mick, you had Sex Kitten. I fancy having a stab at it? She's on now. Have a look. Yeah. I'll ring ya back.'

I am able to keep quiet, but I know my eyebrows have gone into the 'Ride of the Valkyries' to express my thoughts.

I force myself to continue to watch whilst Dougie changes the connectors on his TV and picks up another remote control.

A fifty-year-old man appears on the screen.

Mick says, 'Yeah I've had her. I'll show you what I mean. I looked on the Log. Jock and Jonny B rated her 6 and as I had nothing better to do.'

The screen changes and there is a thirty-something girl straddling Mick. He keeps looking at the camera and winking whilst they have sex.

Dougie complains, 'Could have done with some close ups.'

'Then she'd have known I was filming her,' explains Mick.

'What could she have done about it?' Dougie actually asks.

'Now't, scrawny bitch,' laughs Mick, without any inclination of decency.

'That might have made it more interesting. I like a bit of sport,' quips Dougie.

I take a few seconds to seriously search for a blunt instrument at this point, to give him the sport he so desperately deserves. However, I am riveted by the horror of what human beings can degenerate into. My eyes refocus to their transfixed position.

'You need to be looking for Sasha then. She's a right firecracker. Definite eight and a half. Arse like a peach.'

'No such thing on here. I'm going younger.'

'Good luck with that then. Live chat is calling.'

I am lost for words. Dougie manages to lower the tone even further with, 'I need a piss,' before he jumps up from the sofa.

I step back from the front door and wait around the corner of the house, shaking my head in disbelief, anger and shame, that I didn't realise what a low-life he is and that I have been associated with him.

Dougie returns from the toilet and closes the front door on his way back to the living room.

'Drat!' I realise this will prevent me listening in. I've had a bellyful anyway.

Probably serves me right. Best I know what I'm dealing with though. Should I tell Daisy to be aware of his seediness?

I find my keys in my bag. Dipping below the level of Dougie's window, I shimmy my way along the neighbours' houses, until I am out of the street.

I'll give you sport, I resolve.

CLUBBING
FRIDAY 5TH MAY
11.45 p.m.

Like a moth to a flame, something makes me want to know the full extent of Douglas's misdemeanours. I also want to check that Daisy is not involved. I know he has another after-hours existence, because Luke tells me when he's seen Douglas in the Savannah Club. I just need to know what's really happening. What I saw has unsettled me, almost as much as my diagnosis. Possibly because I didn't have a clue. This is why I find myself in the Savannah nightclub at almost midnight, wearing a short dress and heels, standing on a balcony overlooking a dance floor.

Below me, talking to two young girls, is the Lothario himself.

I'll just try to line up my drink, to see if I can pour it over lover boy's head.

'Oh, blimey!' A man has just pushed past me and dragged my handbag around the post. It's a good job I have the rail to hold me up.

There is another scuffle across the walkway, because a girl has fainted. I can see the people around her are pulling back to give her space. Now two bouncers appear and are giving the girl mouth-to-mouth resuscitation. An ambulance crew have appeared and are lifting the girl onto a stretcher.

She doesn't look well. I can hear people whispering, I decide to get a closer look. I can hear something about, 'You should never have given her that stuff. It's deadly.'

I sidle back to my lookout post. He is still below the balcony, but oh dear, only one little hottie to chat to, now, Douglas.

I notice a large bottle of beer on the table to my right. Picking it up I line it up with his head, below me. The blonde-haired girl leaves him to walk towards the toilet. I think I'll follow her.

I wait for a toilet to become free and Blondie appears at the side of me. Does she know who I am? We both stare into the mirror and I look directly at her.

I then look down into my open handbag. What I see sends me into panic. I immediately close the clutch again. I wait, then enter a toilet cubicle as soon as possible. When inside I open my handbag and take out a parcel of pills, wrapped in a small plastic bag. I climb up onto the window ledge and throw the bag out of the window. It lodges on the windowsill outside. I exit the toilet.

Back in the club: I return to my viewpoint above Douglas and the blonde-haired girl. I can see that they are leaving.

I know this is a waste of time but my curiosity is rampant. I follow them to Douglas's house in my car. Sitting outside until the early hours of the morning I eventually see the girl leave, in a taxi, alone. I'm not sure this is worth the trouble, or why I am putting in the effort. It just feels the right thing to do. As I watch I keep having a flashback to the drugs on the windowsill outside the toilet. I realise I am a stupid woman, because I had the perfect answer for if the pain gets too bad. Why did I throw it out of the window?

RETURNING TO THE DRUGS
SATURDAY 6TH MAY
4.30 a.m.

The dawn is now breaking, my favourite time of day. It occurs to me that I might not be able to sleep through the night in the near future. I return to the Savannah Club and walk around the outside until I see glazed windows. I smile because I can see a small package on the windowsill.

After a breakfast from a well-known food chain, I wait until it is late enough to visit Callum. I decide to visit him and collect the dogs. He is busy so I take the pooches to the park. The puppies ride in a festival trolley as they are still awaiting their jabs and I'm avoiding the vet's. 'I need to get my money out of the bank,' I tell the dogs.

I am too tired to get up much speed. Honey is trotting through the morning dew. There are fishermen at the lake, already set up and organised. One man is using a telescopic net to land his catch. My brain spins into use. I smile.

BACK TO THE CLUB
SATURDAY 6TH MAY
11.00 p.m.

It is 11 p.m. and The Savannah Club is open for business. I'm inside and heading straight for the toilet. Inside the cubicle I pull a small telescopic fishing net from my clothing. Balancing on the window ledge, I can reach out through the open toilet window.

A woman is sighing loudly outside the door.

She bangs on the door. 'Come on, love. I'm plaiting me legs out here. What you doing?'

This is not the only toilet, I think to myself, and then ignore her.

After several attempts I pull the package inside the window. Fastening it in my undergarments, I leave the toilet, scoot down the stairs and exit the club.

On my way out, I notice that Dougie is standing at the bar with a red-haired girl and that he sees me as I leave. *Phew*, I think to myself. But my audacity will aggravate him, I hope.

Out in the street, I walk as quickly as possible without drawing attention to myself.

I hear someone shout, 'Mum'.

I keep walking, not looking back.

'Lauren,' a group of boys shout.

I turn and grin.

My darling son is pleased to see me. He introduces me to his friends. Boys who have grown up at my house over the last nineteen years.

'This is my mum, Lauren.'

They find this amusing too.

'Yes, Luke. How are you, Mrs Laker?'

'Very well thank you, Ryan. It's good to see all of you having such a good time. I'll catch up with you later, Lukey. Be safe.'

Luke is obviously inebriated from drink. I am sort of pleased, because I have an excuse to leave him to his night out... and hide my drug cache. That's something I never expected to say.

I couldn't think of a way to watch Dougie without him spotting my car. So I am taking the bus. Well, I have been taking several buses, over the course of this evening. In fact, I have just met one bus driver for a second time tonight. He is behaving strangely. Maybe he thinks I fancy him?

It is getting a bit boring, but I've just seen Dougie leave his house with a petite brown-haired girl. I push the bell and jump off the bus. Walking back, I can see that Dougie boy is opening the passenger door of his car for Ms Brunette.

Maybe he hasn't had her yet and is trying to impress her. My subconscious stabs me like a pin.

Maybe he really likes her. I'm pleased that this has no effect on me.

Neither does the fact that he's snogging her face off. I am surprised when the passenger door opens and another girl climbs into the back of the car. Now they're driving off. I've left my car down here in the street behind his house. Not my real car, I've hired one. Might as well do the job properly.

OK, we're outside the club now and I can see D. queuing with Ms Brunette. I'm not sure why I'm relaying this information like a commentary, except it feels like I'm narrating a pantomime. I calculate that it's almost twelve midnight, so the longest I'll have to wait for them to reappear is two hours. Best keep out of view. Although if D. were to see me for a fleeting second again, it might really P him off. Is it worth paying the entrance fee?

Yes, but I think I'll have a cup of tea instead. What a good idea to bring a flask. I pour it, making sure I do not rise above the level of the dashboard, except for a crafty sneak to view the entrance of the club. I am aware this is a ridiculous situation.

It's only been twenty minutes when he reappears alone and approaches his car.

Surely, he hasn't dumped her already?

He's climbing into the back of the car for some bizarre reason. A nap perhaps?

Nooooo, surely not, they can't be, can they? The car is unmistakably rocking. I am appalled to a whole new level and transfixed at the bare audacity of the man. What shall I do? Well, really, it's none of my business, I suppose. Except for making sure I never go near him again.

As I turn to sink down in the seat, I notice that Ms Petite Brunette has appeared at the entrance to the club. My mischievous side overwhelms me. After all, everyone needs some entertainment in their lives. Limping across the road, as my leg has gone to sleep and lost its functionality, I approach Petite Brunette. She looks at me with disdain as I wave my hand in an appropriate direction and inform her that, 'Dougie is in his car, waiting for you.'

Ms Brunette stomps off in her stilettos and approaches the car. I can see from her reaction that she has quickly worked out why the car is rocking and the windows are steamed up. She is banging loudly on the window. The driver's door opens and Dougie appears. His solution to the problem shocks all of us, including the bouncers from the club, who have appeared to watch the show.

'Want to come and join us?' he offers feebly, but still audibly to the trained ear... and telescopic microphone. (No, I'm joking. I haven't been out and bought specialist surveillance equipment... yet.)

Despite her diminutive size, Ms B can lift some pretty large rocks.

She is searching around and finds substantial boulders, which she hurls with alacrity at the car. The dents in the BMW are substantial. The bouncers from the club now watch with indifference.

I decide to get the hire car and pull alongside, as though I just happen to be passing.

As I am walking across the road, a car pulls up next to me and the dogs inside are obviously excited to see me. The passenger side window lowers. Callum is beaming. 'We ran out of dog food. They won't eat macaroni cheese any more,' he explains.

It sounds a little like, 'I carried a watermelon,' i.e., contrived, but I'm more than happy to give him the benefit of the doubt, as I am delighted to see him, even though I know I look a mess.

I offer to follow him home, to help to feed the dogs. He agrees to, 'Put the kettle on.'

Back in the carnage, I watch the bouncers pull Ms Brunette off the car and away from Dougie. They direct her back to the club. Dougie is out of the car and making a counter attack to protect his vehicle. This could have got ugly.

I gingerly slide back into the hire car, so as not to make any sudden movements which would reveal my identity. Facing myself in the rear-view mirror, I ask myself two questions:

How could I have been so stupid?

How could I not have known what was going on?

I sink down below the firing line to think strategically and collect my thoughts.

Bobbing up, I can see Dougie standing in the road. There is no one near him, or indeed present in the street any more. I could drive at him now and knock him dead, literally.

I play with the image in my head. How much heartache would I save for my fellow females, including my own daughter?

Ah, Daisy. I imagine a courtroom, with her and Luke crying as I get led away. I remember Callum's cheeky, loving face through his car window. This helps me to swim back to reason.

The woman who has just been performing the back seat athletics is slithering out of the car, so she can wrap herself around Dougie's body, much to his annoyance. She looks familiar, even from this distance.

You're not worth the hassle, Dugless, I tell myself and pull a scarf around my head for disguise, before driving past him.

Down the road I stop to text Callum:

Sorry, really tired, can we make that morning tea instead?

THE START OF REVENGE
SUNDAY 7TH MAY
1.00 a.m.

I decide to take the gamble that Dougie won't return home until after two. That gives me about an hour. I still have his key and let myself into his house, before starting to search his bedroom.

I ask myself, *Surely, someone as thick as him would need to write his password down?*

A car has pulled up outside the house. I freeze.

I grab my bag and run down the stairs. Peeping through the letterbox in the front door, I can see a man and woman walking towards the house next door. I relax.

As I walk back past the living room towards the stairs, the TV pings.

I frantically search for the remote. I turn the TV on and off, but nothing shows.

Again, I hear a 'ping' and follow the direction of the sound. A laptop is slipped under the sofa. When I lift the lid, it springs to life.

Why would you leave it on Dugless? I am perhaps overly suspicious now.

The laptop displays an open dating site. There are several messages from different women.

SUSSY XXX: Shag, sleep, shag, repeat?

HELEN: Can see that you've stayed in tonight. Thank you for waiting for me. Want to come over for some food next week?

Ah now it makes sense. I'm not the only naive idiot out there then?

I start to photograph the messages.

SHAN: I'm really not that kind of girl.

I am intrigued but apprehensive as I scroll back through the messages to find out what he has asked her to do.

DOUGIE DOG: It's me mate's birthday, any chance of us both?

Unbelievable. Not a hint of subtle etiquette. I'm sure he wasn't quite that bad with me. Not in the beginning. But then he did ask me to lend him some money.

Anyway, he hasn't got any mates.

I am aware of the hands of the clock turning. Just a few more peeks.

A fresh Facebook message appears.

CRAZY DAISY: Dougie. I have asked you not to get involved. I can handle it. You know he's my boss. There are procedures to protect employees and I'm big enough to follow them. Please leave things alone or I'll tell Mum.

'I knew there was something wrong. Tell Mum what?' I ask myself.

I close the laptop and slide it back under the sofa. Grabbing my bag, I exit the house. My mind is whirling and I can't concentrate any more.

I need to rest.

MONDAY 8TH MAY

I need to sleep.

THE NEXT ITEM ON THE LIST
TUESDAY 9TH MAY
6.45 a.m.

Now I have one job well underway, it's time to sort another. It's amazing how much information you can still find in a library. Having spent all day yesterday searching through the records of Companies House, to find Daisy's company, I am now tooled up. However, I didn't get much sleep, hence me being here, outside Clive's house at 6.45 a.m. in the morning.

I am watching a middle-aged man (Clive, Daisy's boss) leave his house and getting into his performance car. I plan to follow him in the hire car and watch his every move...

At 8.20 a.m. he enters Samson and Company. I can see Daisy's car also in the car park, so I keep well hidden.

At 11.30 a.m. he drives to a bookmaker's betting office. I see him passing money over the counter, as I enter. I feel conspicuous but no one seems to take any notice of me, despite being one of two females in here, the other being behind the counter. He then returns to work.

It's a long wait until 5.40 p.m. when he leaves the office. I run my phone battery down from being on Google all day searching for information on brain tumours. I start to soften and feel guilty when I follow Clive to the supermarket and he buys flowers and wine. Until I tell myself cynically, there's no guarantee they'll be for his wife.

I am struggling with the prospect of sleeping in the car all night whilst I continue my vigil outside Clive's house. Only I know I'm doing this and quite frankly, I'm starting to feel sorry for myself. I need a break.

The next morning, revived from a full night's sleep, shower and a hearty breakfast, I am back outside the house for 7 a.m. Perhaps by telepathy, I have dressed smartly for the day. Which is fortuitous when at 2.00 p.m., Clive leaves Samson and Company and travels to a gentleman's club on the other side of town. Here my sympathy disappears. Looking at my phone, it is two thirty on Wednesday afternoon.

I am surprised how easily I have walked into this male domain, then realise why and giggle. I can see from my seat in the entrance hall that a young elegant woman in a suit is meeting Clive. She hands him a leather portfolio.

They sit at the bar. I sit at the side of them and take the portfolio, because they are distracted by becoming touchy feely with each other. I leave and immediately photograph the documents in my car. *Bingo, gotcha.*

I return the portfolio and the three hundred pounds in bank notes to the club reception desk, telling them I found the items on the roof of a Jaguar, then leave the building.

I am aware that I may have become too blasé about my new routine, but once again I find it easy. I know it is taking up my precious time, but I want to be thorough. If I'm honest, I also get a kick out of knowing I have the credentials to blend in with the party girls. There isn't one here who isn't attractive.

Satisfied with my successes today, I go home early, to get ready to look casually 'knock out' for Callum. I then remind myself it's a waste of effort and relax.

CALLUM'S HOUSE
TUESDAY 9th MAY
7.20 p.m.

I arrive at Callum's house, after texting to check it is OK. He answers the door immediately, because he wants to share the hilarious antics of the pups. Honey is trying to sleep as the younger dogs are fighting with each other and falling into her.

I push them away and stroke Honey.

Callum makes me a coffee and passes it to me.

'I've come to take them off your hands. You've had them for over a week. I should pay you?' I offer.

He seems genuinely so pleased to see me as he explains they are good company.

He asks if I've finished what I need to do. When I explain I'm well on my way, he asks to have them a few more days, because Honey loves them.

I want to broach 'the' subject and ask if he wants to keep one or two of them, but don't want to bring down the mood.

'You are really kind,' I enthuse.

'But you're thinking, what's the catch?' he offers.

'Not really, I have so many more things to worry about. You know what they say about a friend in need?'

'Is a pest?' he quips. 'I'm a good listener.'

'You are so much more than that,' pops out of my mouth and I start to gabble.

'Work are ringing me. I have self-certificated as long as I can. I need to get a plan together.'

I finish my coffee because I sense the atmosphere may become more intense.

'Thank you, hopefully I can pay you back for your kindness. I've left some cash for the dog food. It's hidden, you'll have to find it and consequently accept it.' I grin.

When he calls me naughty, it makes my pulse race. I wonder if he can tell?

He turns his attention to the dogs. 'Come on guys, say goodbye to mummy!'

The dogs scamper around the kitchen. I catch sight of a vet's bill on the side table, with PAID, amount of £90 for suture to puppy's leg.' I shake my head and smile warmly at Callum, as I leave the house.

BEING THOROUGH
WEDNESDAY 10TH MAY
7.00 a.m.

The next day, I repeat the surveillance of Clive's house, but this time I follow Clive's wife and child (according to the Electoral Roll). They leave in another car. The wife drops off her daughter at play school and I tail the woman to a coffee shop on the outskirts of town. Following her in, I sit near her as she takes brunch with a friend.

Leaving her in the coffee shop, I return to Clive's house and follow the postman as he walks up the path. I take the mail from Clive's letterbox, when the postman has gone. There is nothing of any use today, so I post it back.

BRING ON BUTCH AND SUNDANCE
WEDNESDAY 10TH MAY
4.00 p.m.

I am in my bank. The highly advertised East Main Alliance. I put my card in the machine at the desk and ask for all of my money.

Even though they know I have ten thousand pounds, they are only willing to give me £250 today. If I need an appointment, that's fair enough, but two weeks' time is unreasonable. I ask for the manager, but even that requires more notice. I wonder if men get the same treatment?

They want to know how I will be taking the money. As far as I know, we stopped trading in olive oil when the Romans went back home. They are unwilling to let me carry cash. I think I'm a big enough girl now. When I allude to the fact that they are mugging me, I realise I may have gone too far. I think about how I can publicise the awful way banks treat customers. In my imagination, I can see Robert Redford and Paul Newman shooting their way out of a bank holdup. This keeps me buoyant.

I decide to try another approach. I ring the internet banking service from my mobile phone whilst I am in the bank.

I talk to the reasonable individual at the other end of the phone who always helps me when I need verification. I explain that I'd like the money tomorrow.

'Can you talk to the cashier in the bank to confirm that please?' I say in a very loud voice.

I pass my mobile phone to the cashier.

'It will be in used notes,' she confirms. 'But the safe is closed tonight.'

Result. 'OK. I'll be back in the morning at nine,' I say sweetly.

'We don't open until 9.30.'

I take my bank card and leave, happy to let her have the last word.

A DOUGLAS APPEARANCE
WEDNESDAY 10TH MAY
6.00 p.m.

I leave the bank and walk through the streets. I stop to smell the roses as I walk through the park.

Walking up to my front door, I let myself into my house. Dougie is there, checking through the magazines in my newspaper rack. He is swishing his blond forelock back with one hand and staring at me, with his head tilted to one side.

He has the nerve to ask where I've been!

I snap back, 'Who are you, my dad? How did you get in? I thought you'd given me all your keys back?'

I have a flashback to the rocking car and shudder. Please tell me this isn't a booty call!

'Don't get lippy.' He is slightly aggressive. I don't like his tone. I'm certainly not going to let him see my unrest though.

'Why, you going to kill me?' I ask casually. 'Believe me when I say, that does not bother me.'

I caution myself with a, *Steady. That might be the answer… but not yet.*

'Why are you following me?' he enquires, half pleasant, half threatening.

'When?' I ask, as innocently as possible.

'You're not denying it then?'

'If you tell me when, I'll be able to explain.'

'In the Savannah, Monday night.'

Ah, I tell myself, *he knows nothing, good.* I don't want to spoil any surprises.

'Who was the girl with red hair?' I enquire.

He tries to deny he knows anything about someone with red hair; although he knows I saw him with her. He's wasting my valuable time. I can't be bothered with his clap-trap and cut right to the chase.

I tell him, 'Douglas darling, it doesn't matter... I'm dying.'

'Well, you can't blame me for seeking out some comfort then, if you're leaving me,' he has the affront to say.

I'm cross with myself, because I'm surprised, he manages to turn it around to be about him and I start to show my anger.

It shows when I blast him with, 'Unbelievable! Your mother should be ashamed of raising such a monster.'

He then defends himself by threatening me with his mother, which says it all. I know I'm in a farce and resolve to teach him a lesson once and for all. Bring it on.

In my head, Years and Years are singing, *If You're Over Me.*

To his comment, 'Yes, and she'll kill you herself, if you go near her again.'

I reply, 'Result,' with a tremor in my voice, because this makes me want to laugh. I start to enjoy myself.

He knows this. 'Stop attention-seeking, Lauren. What do you imagine you are dying of?'

'Venereal disease.' I say it quietly and hang my head. Mainly to stop my smirking face from giving the game away.

'As if. You are such a drama queen.' Then after a pause, to allow his brain to catch up, he asks, 'Which one?'

I am deliberately obtuse. 'I know about them all. Blondie from Summergang's Place. Does she ever brush her hair? Bandy legs from Garthorpe. The one who looks like she's constantly chewing a wasp...who likes the back of cars.

'Really, Douglas, can't you find just one person with a modicum of class or grace?'

Other than me, of course.

Douglas stares at me.

'Close your mouth, you look like you're catching flies.'

He is subdued. 'I meant, which venereal disease?'

I bend and whisper in his ear, 'You'll need to have some sort of umbrella test, apparently.'

I turn away from him as I smirk.

'You bitch, I can't believe you've done this to me.'

Even though acting, I am still genuinely incredulous. 'How come you blame me? We haven't had sex in weeks.'

He grabs his leather jacket. His parting shot is how he still believes we had a really good thing going. Well, he did. I pick up a ceramic vase, but he leaves before I can throw it.

He shouts through the letterbox, 'We're done.'

I say to myself, 'You might be, but the fun has just started for me, Goldilocks.'

I can hear I don't give a fuck, as Dua Lipa dances around my head.

Whilst he is still raw, I decide to text Dougie.

LAUREN: *I have a large amount of our savings and I'm not sure who the life policy will go to, as you're not my partner any more.*

I grin wickedly to myself, knowing that I moved all of the money into my account when he bought himself a car, without telling me.

Within seconds there is a returned text.

DUG LESS: *I was your partner when we took the policy out though. How about dinner tomorrow, on me, then we'll talk to a solicitor?*

I tell myself, *In your dreams.* Maybe he's a jellyfish? Completely transparent and no backbone.

Then another text comes through:

DUG LESS: *How long you got?*

Well, that didn't last long. How thoughtful and what a lovely turn of phrase, I comment to myself.

Then a voicemail comes through. It is one of Douglas's floozies. I don't know or care which one. I do sort of, recognise the voice, though.

WITHHELD NUMBER: *I know you are dying, get on with it and leave us alone. He's mine now.*

I reach for my phone, then think better of it. I'm better than this. Why would I want to get embroiled in this level of human interaction?

Half an hour later, it starts again.

DUG LESS: *Why are you being so difficult? Sheree just wants*

to be friends. Leave her alone.

Throughout the night I keep waking with anger, yet managing to stop myself from texting back. In the morning, refreshed from sleep, it all falls into place. I say to myself, *Sorry, Dug less, I don't want to play any 'fight for your man' games with you and your bint. I'm just grateful to her for getting you out of my hair.*

GIVE ME MONEY. THAT'S WHAT I WANT FRIDAY 11ᵀᴴ MAY 9.30 a.m.

Second… no third to dread, after the doctors and dentist is the bank. It takes a lifetime to earn the money and then you have to negotiate the quicksand of changing systems, interest, account types and pain-in-the-neck cashiers to get the money out. My bank, have got customer abuse down to an art form.

If I had more time, I would be willing to appreciate their creative attempts to develop my patience.

However, I haven't. I am not amused as the cashier tells me their safe won't open, again. Really? They want to transfer my money to another bank! My dogged determination is brimming over into thoughts of violence, but I know not to let them see this. At least I hope they can't. I am heading for the door now and an idea skips across my consciousness. Surely the town branch of this bank can't also say their safe is locked… can they? It's worth a try, so I ask for them to transfer my money and miraculously they comply immediately. Now what are they up to?

Exiting the bank, I stomp across the street and enter the solicitors' office opposite, dropping off a copy of my will.

Two hours have passed and I'm now in the main High Street branch of East Main Bank. They have a different excuse of why I can't have my cash. I have no proof of how I've earned the money. In my head I'm in a scene from Robin Hood. The Sheriff of Nottingham is fastened to a tree with arrows. I have a knife in my hand. Back in the real world I decide to make a sharp exit, before I lose the plot and do something I know I'll regret.

Fast forward two more hours whilst I get home, rummage through my filing system and find ten years' worth of wage slips.

'Yes,' I exclaim and lift my fist in celebration.

I actually physically pat myself on the back and give myself a hug. Sad, I know, but I am so pleased with myself. I peer through to the kitchen clock and the time is three fifteen. Does the bank close at four thirty? It's worth a try. I head to my car.

BACK WITH THE HOLE IN THE WALL GANG SATURDAY 12TH MAY 10.50 p.m.

Well, here I am again, waiting at the counter of East Main Bank. My subconscious is keeping my sarcastic self under control, as I push my wage slips forward and smile. 'You need these to prove how I earned my money,' I explain, hopefully without giving away how undignified this makes me feel.

The cashier disappears and I can see her talking to an older woman behind the screen. The cashier returns. 'Your signature does not match the one we have on file'.

'I have several cards with my signature on. It might have changed. I have been with you for nearly thirty years,' I force through gritted teeth. 'Can I see the file with the original one please?'

The cashier flushes bright red. I stifle a grin. *Got you*, I think to myself.

'I, I'll have a look.' She hurries off to the older woman in a suit.

'One moment please?' I call her back. 'Can I just show you, my passport? This is my signature.'

The pow-wow continues behind the screen, even though they know I can obviously see them.

Particularly, as they keep looking across at me. Do they think I will be embarrassed and back off, I wonder? Is this bullying? I definitely feel uncomfortable. It is definitely intentional and repeated. I ask myself again, would they do this to a man? A 'man' appears. He is called over to the secret discussion. The cashier scuttles off and returns with what looks like a large envelope.

Cashier Kate (the younger) comes back to my area of the desk and empties ten plastic bags full of twenty-pound notes onto the counter.

I look behind me to see the long queue which has formed. It doesn't even look like that much money, but I am shocked at the total lack of security or consideration.

I stare at her incredulously but this has no affect.

'Could we perhaps do this in private?' I ask as sarcastically as possible.

'I don't know if there are any rooms free,' Katie cashier replies indifferently.

'Perhaps there?' I point my finger directly at the room opposite, which is clearly being vacated by an older couple.

'It might be booked.'

'Yes, it might', I agree and turn my back.

In my mind I am in a sketch from the *Two Ronnies*. The queue, which is now some fifteen people, has become the audience. Maybe it's the tumour taking hold?

Behind me I hear Katie cashier saying, 'OK. Booth four is available.'

After a protracted wait, I follow her and the older woman across to booth four.

I half expect it to be full of police and remember Mrs Walters at the doctors' surgery.

I wait to be invited to sit down, just to demonstrate that I have more manners than them. In the unlikely event that they know what manners are.

'We weren't sure we had ten thousand pounds,' states the older woman.

If I was losing the plot, this brings me sharply back into focus. 'Are you the main bank for this larger-than-average town?' I enquire.

'What are you going to spend it on?' she asks sweetly, rudely refusing to answer my question.

'What I want,' I reply curtly, not taking the charmed bait.

'What are you going to spend it on?' she demands.

'My funeral.' The words spill out before I can stop them. Both the woman laugh. Possibly from shock, but if so, rottweiler soon recovers. They are buzzing about the prospect of getting rid of me.

In my mind, I can see Mrs Walters frantically shaking her head. The *Two Ronnies* are crying. I hope my face remains expressionless. Eventually Butch and Sundance appear in my mind and hold up some dynamite for me to see.

'You won't need ten thousand for that,' older woman chirps. 'Leave some in your account.'

Sundance hands me the dynamite and I laugh. This unnerves the two women. I am pleased with myself, because I haven't started taking any drugs yet and I'm still managing to gain my mental control back. I continue to smile enigmatically.

'We only have used notes,' she apologises, but with little conviction.

'That's fine.' I'm not sure I'd believe newly made ones would be legitimate from these specimens, I contemplate to myself.

Cashier Kate counts the packs of a thousand in front of me and older woman.

'Would you like me to get you a large envelope?' she offers, as though I am her mate!

'No, thank you.' I pack the plastic bags into a carrier bag in my rucksack and try not to look like a hamster let loose in a peanut farm.

Butch Cassidy rides past me on his bike in the sunshine and offers me the cross bar. I decline but follow him out of the building. As I walk down the street my eyes stream with tears. I steady my body by clutching the bag and set my resolve.

MY GIRL
SATURDAY 12TH MAY
7.45 p.m.

With the carrier bag labelled 'Daisy' and 'Luke' safely stashed away, I return to my 'to do' list.

It is early evening as I enter this busy pub and stand behind a man at the bar. He is waiting to get served but there are so many people pushing through that he hasn't noticed me. Good. I find the largest man I can see on the other side of the bar and grin mischievously at him. Oo-er, this could all go terribly wrong.

My heart is pounding, but once I get into action it suspends any blood flow so I can think. I like this new me.

I lean forward and push myself against Clive. He doesn't seem to notice or perhaps he doesn't mind. I lean to whisper in his ear, 'Don't turn around. That enormous giant of a man to your right works for me.'

I know he can hear me because he looks at Man Mountain across the other side of the bar. Man Mountain is probably a nice man and I do feel a little bit guilty for this subterfuge. I also don't want him coming over at this moment. So I hurry up.

'I know all about your trips to The Peppermint Pig, the gambling and the debt mounting up in your secret bank accounts. The bank accounts, in your wife's name.'

'Who are you?' Clive shouts and tries to turn, until I stick a pin in his leg and push him against the bar. He lets out a cry of pain, so I fake a sneeze to cover the noise. I have thought this through, but try not to become too pleased and complacent. A girl at the side of us takes advantage and pushes forward in the jam which should be a queue. He is wedged conveniently, so I continue.

'Aren't daughters wonderful?'

'I have a lovely little girl, too. She works for you. You bully her. You sexually harass her. Daisy Laker. Greg, over there to your right, works for you, and also me, now. He's going to let me know when Daisy receives the promotion she so rightfully deserves. Do you understand?'

Clive is nodding and slowly starts to turn around. By this time, I am hyperventilating out in the street and he will be finding a high stool wedged into his back.

This was far too easy to be effective, but not even slightly fun. I just felt I had to do it.

Another one down. Now to use my practise run for the real thing.

I get an invitation to dinner from Callum. I feel guilty. I don't know why. But I do want to go. He doesn't know I'm losing my mind and he is sooo cute, so I reply.

LAUREN: *Love to.*

GETTING CREATIVE
SUNDAY 13TH MAY
11.00 p.m.

I'm in Dougie's house. Fortuitously, I still have a set of keys. My low profile has paid off because he hasn't had the good sense to change his locks. Oh excellent, no one in the building. His living room is relatively tidy. Perhaps he's had a French maid around? Who cares?

I have a strong desire to Google 'How to get even when your man cheats,' but feel this would leave a footprint on the iCloud, which might incriminate me. So I've remembered a few ideas from what friends have told me over the years. Can't bring myself to cut up his clothes, though. Don't want to give him a chance to update his wardrobe, when he looks so Worsel Gummidge all by himself. Oh, how the criminal mind works. I have no guilt about lover boy, maybe because I know him too well.

However, this very reasonably priced grass with wildflower seed and fertilizer will dramatically improve his carpet. Make it all so alfresco in here. Let's just give it a little water to start it off. Oh, go on then, one more visit to the tap. Luckily, he hasn't put locks on his windows. I'll just throw this watering can into the garden.

Now let's add a little coastal aroma to enhance the mood even more. Prawns in the finials, sir? No, I always walk like this, officer. Ha, Ha, ha. In my head, Ronnie and Ronnie applaud.

Upstairs, I head for the bedroom. Umm, knickers, or pants, I suppose. What have I got for these? Do I have time to check out my array of substances? No need, here it is. Prime joke shop itching powder.

And through to the bathroom.

'I never did like this toothpaste.' I present to the mirror. 'But we do like this one'.

Amazing how easily the top comes off. Like I am meant to refill it with fart goo. I take the toothbrush and give it a good scrub around the toilet lip.

It's a shame to waste good Calvin Klein, but hey ho, the bottle is leering at me from the bathroom cabinet. Down the loo and then, after a little comfort break, refilled with eau de toilette it is.

I can't waste time now. I'm on a roll and don't want to get caught. However, the hair remover cream pops to the top of my bag, just begging to be appreciated. How could I have overlooked this? If I lose my hair and this is highly likely, the one way to stop Dugless from harassing me is to put him in the same position.

As I am leaving by the front door, I sweep my eyes across the living room. 'He'll never know I've been,' I tell myself. 'Until the grass grows in his carpet. Or his balls start to itch.'

It was this thought that woke me at five this morning. It continually aggravates me, and I have to ask myself, do I want to waste any more time on him?

'I so do,' I tell myself as I stare in the mirror and check the stability of my hair roots.

I am slightly deflated as I walk along the street from Dougie's house. Maybe I should install a camera, so I can watch his reactions as he realises how his life has become less comfortable? Probably best not to go back in there now, though. I giggle to myself, but at the back of my mind, I'm thinking he probably won't even notice.

Back at my house, my computer whirs into action. I find an awful picture of Doug and upload it onto a new profile on his favourite dating site. I call it 'SO SORRY.'

Typing like a banshee because I am engrossed by the task, I write:

I would like you all to know that I have a serious sexually transmitted disease and that you should get yourselves checked as soon as possible.

I am also sorry that we have been filming you having sex with us and sharing this with others on this site:

Togerheaven.fishingforfun@aol.co.uk

I wished I could have given you bigger ratings out of ten but I prefer young, thin girls.

I love you all. Dougie.

My address is: 75 Gatacre Road, Whinthorpe WN8 7TP

I type the address, then remove it. Then type it again.

I tag all the girls on the site from my list of names from his phone and his old account and send the message.

Lying back on my bed, a self-satisfied smile makes me forget for a while that I have other more terminal problems.

DINNER AT CALLUM'S
SUNDAY 13TH MAY

I am on a relative high, as I follow Callum through to his kitchen. It is six o'clock, which is early for a dinner date, but I'm pleased because I'm starving.

As I come back from the toilet, I see four bowls lined up with dog treats in them. They have the names painted on them: Honey, Foxy, Sox and Piglet. It makes me smile.

Callum comes into the hall. He is awkward.

'I'm sorry, they don't have to keep these names if you don't like them,' he offers.

I am staring as thoughts fly through my head.

'Maybe we should have named them together?' he asks. I continue to stare.

Like a family? I am thinking, but I dare not utter the words. How am I going to tell him what's happening to me, when he has just lost his mum?

I smile at him and follow him to the kitchen table.

'So we've had longer to get to know each other now?' he opens.

'Yes.' I smile.

'So… I find myself wanting to get to know you and what you get up to when you're away. You're going to tell me, "not much," aren't you?' He laughs.

'Quite the contrary,' I say, 'I'm always up to mischief.'

I grin.

'Are you still with the laddo?'

'Douglas? No.'

'Not Dougie?'

'He hates Douglas, so I always use it. I tell him his mother insists.'

'That sounds like a lot of work to me.'

'Yes, a waste of life.'

'I am probably prying. What I mean is… It's been a long time since I've been interested in anything, since my mum died.'

'Oh.' I try not to panic.

Callum busies himself, straining the vegetables and tipping them into a large dish.

We eat slowly and keep smiling at each other.

I leave a third of the food on my plate, because I'm worrying about where this conversation is going to lead. How much do I tell him?

Callum leans over to take my plate and our hands touch momentarily. I pull away. Why did I do that?

Callum smiles.

I follow him into the kitchen and go for it.

'Callum, I'm not being evasive,' I tell him.

'Can we sit down for a minute?'

We sit opposite each other. I take his hands.

'I'm dying. I have a brain tumour. Sod's law really. First time I find someone I like and they seem to like me back.'

He seems suspended in a daze. Eventually he realises he is back in the moment.

'What's that Alanis Morrissette song?' he asks,

'I won the lottery and died the next day.'

How does he know about Alanis? Why is he being so calm?

But that's a good thing, right?

He pulls me towards him and holds me against his chest. It feels so good. He smells delicious. I am starting to imagine dying in his arms.

'Shush. It doesn't matter,' he whispers. 'I had an inclination it was something like that.'

He wipes a tear away. His face changes although it is still kind.

I realise the objectivity is to protect me. I try to explain. 'I didn't want to tell you, so soon after your mum dying.'

'It's just so unfair. You are so young. Do you mind me asking how long you have?'

'No idea. Daren't go back to ask, even if I could get through the appointment system. I'm scared I'll throttle the receptionist. Or give her any satisfaction.'

'Go to another doctor,' he suggests. 'Go to mine, they're good. At the very least get a second opinion?'

I agree, 'OK.' At this moment I would probably promise him anything.

'I'll come with you,' he offers. 'I know you're thinking too much, too soon, but things happen like that sometimes. I wish I could have done more for my mum. It would make me feel so much better, having something positive to concentrate on.'

I can't believe he is so sweet but know his needs are also important now. He is fragile. I want to panic and feel overwhelmed, but somehow, I don't. Instead, I want to be strong for him.

The warm glow of realisation spreads over me, as I feel less alone. Then reality bites.

'But...' I add.

'What?'

'What about after? When you're alone again? It will be like grieving twice.' I have to be honest with him.

I have to go, to clear my head and to give him the chance to back away.

The dogs sense there is something wrong. Sox and Piglet nuzzle me as I grab my coat and leave.

'I just want to give you some space,' I whisper, as I head out of the door.

He calls after me calmly, 'Don't give up. You don't have to do this on your own.'

I believe him and return to hug him again. 'Thank you.'

POSITIVITY
MONDAY 14TH MAY
8.30 a.m.

The next morning, I find myself in bed and remarkably refreshed. I've slept well. The ping of my mobile wakes me. Maybe Callum hasn't slept. He's straight on the case.

CALLUM: *Can I explain to my doctor about your situation?*

I return the text:

Yes, better than doing nothing. My firm are breathing down my neck. They may start sending out a missing person's release soon, if I don't make contact. I need to talk to Daisy and Luke first, though (My children). My ex (not my children's father) is performing his usual self-obsessed idiot routine.

I send the reply and sit up in bed. This is reality then. Time to face up to the truth.

I don't mention that I've already been pulled by my boss and had a 'heart to heart appraisal' about my missing persona. Apparently even when my body has been present, it has seemed like my mind has not. I didn't like to tell her that my creativity is what keeps getting our clients out of bother. However…

Another text comes through from Callum.

Dr Watman at 1.30 p.m. Tomorrow.
18, Sandringham Street, GN8 4AS.
Sure you don't want me to go with you?
I text:
Will make sure I'm there. Prob. best by myself, but thanK you. XX

CALLUM: *Good Luck, XXX*

I drift off to sleep, in which Callum and I are running along a sandy beach and splashing in an azure tropical ocean.

***

5 p.m.

A car hoots. Outside my house the neighbour's childcare client has blocked the entrance to my drive again. I ask her to move, as I may have an emergency at any minute. My neighbour yells out of her window like the fishwife she is, 'She's got a licence, she can park where she likes.'

I look at them both laughing at me, and stare at them, a front, whilst behind my eyes, my brain is in full planning mode. I wait until the woman straps her child into their car and leaves the street. Nonchalantly, dropping back behind her car, I follow her to her home. I smile sinisterly at how easy it has been to find revenge and teach her some much-needed manners.

At well past midnight I return to the childcare woman's house. There is no moon. In sneakers I quietly fetch every wheely bin in the street and gradually, starting from just outside her front and back door, which are fortunately next to each other; I wedge the big black lumps of plastic into a pleasing pattern. Most of them are full and quite frankly, stink. In the morning, when she is rushing to work, she will have to either ring someone to help her move them, or climb out of her window to leave her house. I make sure my hood is always well pulled down over my head and walk like a navvy, for added disguise. Just in case I make the TV news again.

A START
TUESDAY 15TH MAY
1.20 p.m.

These places make me shiver, even with a jumper and a coat wrapped around me. I'm waiting for feedback from the doctor's receptionist. She is friendly and professional. Sadly, this shocks me. Here it comes. I approach the desk.

Ah, seems they need my notes. That's going to cause an issue for sure, although hopefully I don't let them see this, by my reaction.

I'd better go and explain to Callum.

***

Waiting outside his door, after ringing the bell, I can see him corralling the escapist dogs. Great things, these glass doors. He is so fit. All I want to do when I see him, is get wrapped in his arms.

In my imagination I can see him embracing me and smelling my hair. I have an image of being bald and have to hold back a sob in my throat.

'How did it go?' he asks gently as he opens the door to me.

I explain that they were sympathetic and efficient but they said it could take up to three weeks to get my files.

I don't feel like waiting around. I don't trust my surgery staff to send them either.

I have a plan, but keep it to myself.

DOING THE DEED
WEDNESDAY 16th MAY
1.00 a.m.

The alarm is set for 1 a.m. When it goes off, I am already awake and pulling on my pre-chosen clothes, all of them black.

I don't particularly remember the journey to my own doctor's surgery, but I am soon here and crow-barring the emergency exit open. My hand, covered by a surgical glove, slips inside. I push the bar and the door opens.

I find the surveillance cameras and turn them on. The emergency door on the screen is still closed. They are obviously not connected.

I still don't hang about. Pulling the cabinet open, I search through the files. Shockingly they are actually in alphabetical order. The 'L' section is in the second drawer down.

The head torch keeps falling over my eyes, which is most annoying. So is the fact that there is no file for Laker.

Whispering to myself I ask, 'I must have notes, where are they?'

One filing cabinet is locked. Searching through the desk drawers and along the top of cabinet, I can continue to watch the images on the security cameras. Just in case, I photograph the cameras using my phone.

Eventually my will strengthens and I decide to take the crowbar to the cabinet. It easily forces open. A large bunch of keys is wedged at the front of the drawer. It contains what looks like, several mementoes. On the keyring there are two grubby tiny teddy bears, a plastic fob, with a photograph of two people, one, Amy, the acid receptionist and the other a man, who has clearly dodged out of sight, as the photograph is taken; a key ring with the name AMY in bright pink plastic and a token to gain access to a shopping trolley.

Right at the front of the drawer is an envelope. It contains some blond hair and a card that says, Happy Birthday, let's celebrate D. Someone has written the sentence, 'forevva mine', on the envelope, and in the same handwriting on a piece of paper which is attached to the files, the word 'burn', is scrawled across it, although the handwriting makes me misread it as 'bum' initially. There are several box files marked in red ink: Case 1, Case 2, Case 3.

I open Case 3. Even I am surprised by what I find.

It makes me step back and gasp, before dropping to the floor, reaching across for my phone and starting to photograph the notes.

After two hours I look at the clock on the wall to see it is half past three. As I start to return the files in an attempt to tidy away, some drop down flat. As I straighten them, I see a file bearing my name, lying on the bottom of the drawer. Snatching it, I start to read.

One sheet has a winking emoji face drawn on it and the name has been obscured using thick black felt pen. In an attempt to ensure my escape with the files, I fold them, and push them into my rucksack. Quickly, I check my previous photograph against the security cameras, mainly to put my mind at rest, when I have left the building.

As I thought, not even these work. I make a praying motion, in thanks.

An immense sense of urgency overtakes me and I flee. Returning to grab the crow bar.

It is just gone 4 a.m. when I get home. The dawn is starting to break and a few trail-blazing birds are breaking the blissful silence and heralding the start of the day. The air smells divine. I feel so alive. The irony does not escape me.

I know I can fall asleep at any time. I feel like a lion having dragged its food back to its secret lair. It is only the desperation of finding out about my tumour that keeps me awake.

However, there is nothing particularly useful written in my notes.

Mumps when I was eighteen, and a catalogue of immunisations from childhood. Details about giving birth, twenty-two and nineteen years ago. Then very little else, except a smear test five years ago. Maybe there are pages missing?

I shudder at the thought of going back there. I can't. Neither do I want to spend my remaining days behind bars.

Taking my phone from my pocket, I realise the battery is low. Climbing the stairs feels like Mount Everest, but I need the charger. Or at least I think I do, until I see the bed. Managing to plug the phone in before I sprawl across the welcoming sheets, I fall into an unconscious state, immediately.

***

Three hours later, I wake and plod steadfastly down the stairs to fetch a pad and pen. Returning to bed I read through my photographs of other people's files and start to make notes. What I read makes me blow with the severity of the information.

On the top of some sheets are the words:

Crown Prosecution case against Doctors Reece, Witherson and James: pertaining to mis-diagnosis of Alzheimer's Disease.

Then another says cervical cancer; another Parkinson's disease.

The mobile pings and makes me halt.

It's Callum, sounding urgent. *Ring me please.*

Oh, I can certainly do that. I immediately comply.

'Good morning,' I say.

'The doctor has rung. He can't talk to me, do you want to ring him?' Callum asks.

'Don't want to, but I know I should,' I reply. 'I will. Thank you.'

As I ring the doctors' surgery, I decide to sit down to take the call. I lay flat and breathe deeply before sitting up and ringing Callum again.

'Hi, they've got me an appointment for a brain scan this afternoon. Did you have anything to do with this?'

'I...'

'Thank you. If it's cost you money, I will pay you back.'

'Can I come with you?'

I imagine sinking into his arms.

'Thank you. Yes. You are good to me.'

He laughs warmly.

THE REVEAL
THURSDAY 17TH MAY
1.45 p.m.

We're sitting in the waiting area. I'm wearing one of those suspect theatre gowns, trying to keep the mood light.

No looking at my bottom if I flash. It won't be intentional.

Callum giggles, it is one of the sexiest sounds I have ever heard.

You've still got your sense of humour then?' he asks.

It's making no difference to me at the moment,' I honestly admit.

I am invited to lie on the bed as they prepare me for a full body scan. The nurse steps back and the machine carries me into the observation tunnel. It stops.

From somewhere outside I hear the radiographer ask, 'Are you humming?'

Oops. 'Sorry. Quiet now,' I offer.

The machine starts to move again.

'Total stillness, please.'

It feels like an eternity before the whirring sound stops and I am released from the capsule. No one comments. I am helped down and sit on a chair in an adjoining room. I dress and return to Callum. He takes my hand.

The silence between us is comfortable. I realise I have never really felt this with another human being before. Not as an adult anyway. I try not to think too deeply as we await the results.

After well over an hour, the doctor returns. I am expecting a nurse to bring the results, so this does not look good.

'This way please.' The doctor, consultant rather, holds the door for me to go through to his office. My heart is pounding. I can hear the blood rushing around my veins and past my ears.

Callum looks and I nod eagerly for him to come with me. We sit together, like two naughty children in a head teacher's study.

Callum takes my hand and squeezes it.

The doctor stares me in the eyes and starts to talk. 'I don't know how to say this.'

'Just do, please,' I plead, bordering on pathetic.

'There are absolutely no signs of any growth or malignancy. You are completely healthy.'

I stare at him.

'Look.' He recognises my disbelief and stands to turn on a screen, which shows the images from the scan.

'I've had two colleagues have a look to make sure. That's why I was so long.'

Even though Callum is watching me, I cannot stem the flow of water, which is streaming down my face.

'I'll give you some time alone.' The doctor quietly leaves his office.

'Oh dear,' is all I can say.

'What? Aren't you pleased?' asks Callum, shocked at my response.

I stand to look at the images. I stroke one.

'Of course, I am. It's just such an emotional time for me.'

'Yes, a veritable bloody roller coaster,' he adds.

'I love my beautiful brain. But it might have got me into lots of trouble.'

I stare at the floor as flashbacks come flooding in:

In a few short seconds I recall almost dropping a bottle onto Dougie's head.

Sticking a pin in Clive's back.

Driving my car past Dougie and almost knocking him over.

Dougie's mother and father fighting.

Falling out of the Savannah Club toilet window and smuggling drugs.

Police almost finding me following Clive's wife.

Lynch mobs shouting at Dougie's door.

Dougie's hair falling out as he looks in the mirror.

A high-speed chase, with the pups in the mobility scooter.

Dougie squealing when he walks in his living room and finds a meadow.

And my boss's face when I called her a talentless gremlin.

The joy overtakes me. Callum is grinning. Thank heavens he can't read my mind. He hugs me and we waltz around the room.

'Then we'll have to use your beautiful brain to get you out of trouble. You're just in shock.'

'Can we go back to yours please? Then do you fancy coming on holiday?'

He laughs heartily.

***

Back at Callum's house, the dogs are definitely feeling the positive mood. We walk them together, in the park. It is a magical, warm, bright evening. My hand feels small in his. We keep looking at each other and smiling.

***

When we return, we start to chat.

'I don't understand how it could have happened?' he asks.

'Things just do sometimes,' I offer.

'Do you want something to happen now?' His voice deepens and it makes my insides perform a pirouette.

'Like a celebration you mean? Yes, I've felt it for ages but didn't want to complicate things. Death makes you want to affirm you are alive.' I don't look up at him because I know my eyes will signal the depth of my lust.

'I can't think of a more reckless affirmation than a kiss.' He bends towards me and the moment seems suspended in time. Maybe because I'm holding my breath. Intoxicated by the euphoria, his gentleness extends my heightened awareness.

It feels so right. Safe and yet, not quite so. We move through the house using furniture and eventually the bed to confirm our relationship. Like doing a high five with all of your senses and body parts. The unity of our bodies in continuous harmony.

Afterwards I'm too high on love and life to sleep. I watch Callum as he breathes beside me. A part of my sensible self wants to issue a warning that no man this beautiful is going to stay around for long. But the child in me slaps the adult's legs. Surely, I should know that miracles do happen.

I stare at the ceiling when he wakes, so he doesn't feel self-conscious.

'You, OK?' he enquires.

'Not sure, let's just check.' I giggle.

I kiss him, all over and return to lie in his arms. My favourite place.

I feel so alive.

I run through different reasons to be grateful. I am SO glad I didn't tell Daisy and Luke. All that pain, for nothing.

'You mentioned your ex before. Does he know?' Callum enquires. I want to tell him he has nothing to worry about, but don't want to confess anything about my acts of revenge.

'That I was dying? Yes. He said I was selfish for leaving him.'

'Joking, right?'

'No. But I told him I was dying of an STD. If I'd have told him brain tumour, he might have tried to have me sectioned. He's not one to miss an opportunity. I might have mentioned I had a life policy though. But I haven't. So he will be looking for me... probably.'

'Are you always so...'

'Negative? I prefer to call it realistic. However, I'm rapidly changing my point of view. How would you feel about tutoring me some more?'

'You might have to stay under my watchful eye,' he states as he kisses my face.

'I might like that.' I fold myself, into the closeness of his body with excitement and pleasure.

'Will he come around here?'

This makes me laugh. 'Not if he thinks I am dead. Besides he doesn't know where you live.'

'Is that what you want him to think?

'Not sure yet. I'm a little overwhelmed at the moment.'

'He must have had some good features?'

'One of my deepest regrets about dying was that I wouldn't be around to see him lose his beloved hair. Other than that, no.'

I have a wicked image of Dougie holding handfuls of hair, which are coming away from his scalp. I smile to myself.

'At least my brush with fate has made me realise not to squander my time.'

'Bit of a harsh way to learn the lesson though,' he states.

'Goes around, comes around. Karma rules, baby.'

'I love how forgiving you are.' He smiles.

***

When Callum leaves the room to visit the toilet, I play *Do I Love You? Indeed I Do* by Frank Wilson on my phone. The dogs join in with the dancing, in their own style, of course.

Callum returns and sits on the bed, watching us and laughing.

There is a knock at Callum's door. I am concerned and ask, 'Stephan perhaps?'

Callum reassures me with a shake of the head, laughing, 'Hope not.'

He grabs a towel and runs down the stairs, returning within minutes. I hear him bounding, three steps at a time back up the stairs. He bounces onto the bed and uncurls, with his arms behind his head, lying there with a happy grin.

'I left the door of the cupboard in mum's bedroom open', he explains. 'Piglet is not one to let an opportunity go to waste.'

I stop my dancing and look cautiously at Callum.

'There were some newspaper cuttings and notes, which must have been taped under the drawer. They were about a man who had been a war criminal. A man who looked very much like Stephan.'

'No,' I utter as I climb onto the bed and stare into his eyes. 'is that what is keeping him away? Have you told him you know?'

'Not yet. I haven't needed to. I was researching international criminal law on the computer in the study, when he turned up at the window, for a ritual haunting. The dogs were in the garden. Honey took one look at him and let's just say, we saw another side to her nature. Of course, the pups came to her assistance. He hasn't been back since.'

'Well let's just hope he doesn't throw something poisonous, over the fence.'

'Good point!' Callum replies, looking concerned.

LIFE AS WE KNOW IT
FRIDAY 18TH MAY
10.00 a.m.

I decide some retail therapy is in order and find myself having a meaningful interaction with a clothes-rail when a woman comes and stands right in front of me. As they do from time to time. Usually, I ignore it and have been known to move away, to avoid confrontation. Not today.

'Certainly,' I state.

'What?' asks the woman, puzzled that she can't do exactly as she wants.

I enlighten her. 'I will excuse you for pushing in front of me,' I explain.

'Didn't ask you to,' she retorts.

I hit her with my substantially sized hips and she flies sideways across the floor.

'No, you didn't, did you?' I confirm.

'I was only looking.' She tries for the sympathy vote as she extracts herself from the pile of clothes she has created.

'So was I,' I state dispassionately.

MANNERS!
FRIDAY 18TH MAY
10.30 a.m.

Feeling I have had my say, I make my way to the coffee shop. There are two old men sitting in the window, relaxing in armchairs and laughing about their friend.

It is delightful to listen to them.

'He always manages to get himself into trouble,' the first old man giggles.

'I told him to get rid of the sideboard and get a coffee table instead.'

They obviously think it is funny, but no one else does. That makes it even, more amusing.

'On that note, I'd better go and find Ada.' Old Man One shakes the hand of his friend. They are celebrating their friendship and a love of life. It makes me smile.

I ask the girl at the café till for a vegetarian sausage sandwich. She informs me that they have run out, as have the supermarket. I find this hard to believe, but change my choice to eggs.

I turn my attention, along with everyone else, to two elderly women who have made quite an entrance into the café. Intent as they are, on gaining the optimum impact, to ensure they have their every need is met. One of them sidles across, to Old Man Two, who has committed the heinous crime, of not looking up from his newspaper.

'I want that seat,' she demands. 'I've got a bad back.'

Old Man Two, gets up and moves to another table. He looks embarrassed.

I swing around to face the Old Woman. She stares at Old Man Two.

I'm not having this! I swing around on my heel.

'Wait a minute,' I say gently to Old Man Two. 'You don't have to move just because she wants something.'

I look around the café, everyone, has stopped to watch. Two people catch my eye and nod their agreement.

'I've got a bad back,' the woman explains to me, with much more respect than before.

'Perhaps, but the world doesn't revolve around you, and there are ways to ask. That was just rude.'

There is an awkward silence and then everyone goes about their business.

The rude old woman approaches Old Man Two and apologises.

Everything settles down as I eat my sandwich.

As I leave the café, I nod to Old Man Two and he winks back.

Before I leave the supermarket, I take a basket and fill it with every type of vegetarian sausage they sell.

There are at least six different makes. I return to the café and leave them on the end of the till counter.

Through the window outside I can see all the café staff talking about the basket and why it has appeared. Well, they'll know where to look when they put them back now, won't they?

I'm on a roll. Time to finish what I started. First, I need to balance my account.

ROBIN HOOD
FRIDAY 18TH MAY
11.45 a.m.

I cross over the street and walk a little way to East Main Bank. It is lunchtime. I am standing in the queue to get served. A man and woman are anxiously waiting behind me. There are four places for cashiers and only two of them are manned. One of the cashiers is slowly counting notes into her till, a few at a time. She looks at her nails in between each task.

A man in a suit appears from a back office, looks at the queue of eight people and disappears back into the office.

The other cashier is waiting for something.

I start to video the cashiers. Eventually they spot me and shout rudely across.

'What are you doing?' demands the cashier.

I shout back just as loudly, to ensure my lack of respect carries across the building.

In my mind's eye, I imagine Mrs Walters. She is applauding me.

'I'm filming how long it takes to get served,' I explain, in a very loud voice.

'You can't do that,' comes the retort from Cashier One. I can hear the waver in her voice.

'Is there a manager in today? Get him for me please. Why isn't he on the desk at this busy time?'

'Yes, I will get him.' She disappears through the door to the back office.

Cashier Two is working so quickly by now that I am about to get served.

Cashier One returns and beckons me forward.

I ignore Cashier One and hand over some cash and my card to Cashier Two.

The manager appears and looks along the queue, searching for me. As his eyes find me at the desk, he looks away.

I pronounce at the top of my voice, 'That's fine, I've sorted the problem myself. I'll send the video to the complaints department and put it on the internet. Good day.'

As I leave the bank, I give myself a talking to, because I know my good luck can't last forever and I want to spend my last few drops on something meaningful and necessary.

You know what's wrong with you. Sort it out, I say to myself.

STAKEOUT
SATURDAY 19TH MAY
8.00 a.m.

I decide to watch my original doctors' surgery from my car. I've been here for three days now and no sightings whatsoever. I can't go into the building. It would leave an evidence trail.

A postman walks past and hangs his coat up in the back of his van. My mind whirs with activity. My plan B.

The mobile pings. The message reads:

DAISY: *Mum, could do with a chat. You about?*

Ignoring the text for now, I walk casually across and take the coat, a hat and an empty post-bag from the post van. I walk behind another larger van and after dressing myself in my new props, I enter the surgery.

'Recorded delivery for Amy Grice,' I state. I think to myself how easy it is to find people on the internet nowadays.

I'm told by the girl behind the desk that Amy has left.

'Have you got her address?' I ask. 'I have to drop this recorded letter off or I get a fine.'

'Sorry, we can't give out addresses,' states the new girl behind the desk.

I scan her face for any clues to whether I could bribe her, but again want to leave a clean trail... if this turns into a murder enquiry.

LIFE GOES ON
SATURDAY 19TH MAY
1.00 p.m.

It is rare that Daisy rings me to meet up. I am delighted as I head to the coffee shop, once I have returned the postman's coat and bag, of course.

Daisy runs to me and hugs me. I am immediately concerned. What has she heard?

'What's wrong?' I ask.

'Nothing, quite the opposite. I've got a promotion... It's in London, though.'

Daisy looks radiant. I congratulate her on her new post, but want to know how it has come about? She explains that her boss, the delectable Clive, is desperate for her to be promoted, but before he spoke to her about his thoughts, she had found her own place. Apparently, because she is so fed up with his attitude. I was right on the nail, then?

I grin as I state that, 'It's funny how things turn out,' without a hint of confession on my lips. Then the conversation turns to Dougie. Daisy knows me well. I hope I am hiding my delight and try to look concerned, when she tells me, he is in trouble.

She asks if I've seen my low-life ex? That's easy on the lie detector.

'No, not for a while,' I offer. Well, I haven't actually seen him, have I?

Daisy tells me, 'He's acting really weird and there are loads of women outside his house.'

'Strange,' I offer, keeping it short so as not to incriminate myself. But I've half a mind to confess to her. If she knows she'll be able to keep herself safer.

'And every time I see him, he has a ridiculous hat on.'

A smirk crawls across my face, as I think of him with a bald head. I turn away to blow my nose. 'Bald heads are sexy on some men,' I offer. 'Although I can't see Douglas being a fan.' Daisy stares into my eyes. I realise she has said nothing about him being bald.

When she asks if I think he has lost it because he has told her that marigolds are growing in his carpet, I can contain myself no longer. She then asks, 'Does he mean washing up gloves?' I can tell by the tone of her voice that she is piecing the evidence together, then realisation beams on her face.

'Mum?' she asks, whilst watching my face. (I can't control my upwardly mobile eyebrows).

I blurt out my confession 'I've done some really awful things to him, Daisy.'

'Are you feeling guilty?' she asks innocently.

I reflect for a few seconds as she stares into my face.

'No,' I bluntly reply, with a deadpan expression. 'Actually, I'm really pleased with myself.'

We both erupt into fits of laughter.

'Mum, he *so* had it coming. I don't know how you've kept so patient with him.'

'Because I haven't known what was going on. Call me old-fashioned, but I believe the best in people. I cannot believe how badly behaved he is. I'm embarrassed to be associated with him, and ashamed I didn't know.'

She is delighted and I get my second hug of the day.

'Thank heavens,' she enthuses. 'There are loads of rumours flying around about him. You're best out of it. I've deleted him from Facebook.'

I grin and nod.

'And I have another confession. I have someone else. Callum,' I say. It sounds so good.

She continues, 'He is a master of bullshit, Mum. My mates are having bets on which one of us he will hit on next.'

'And he has a far, far, far too big an opinion of himself,' I state.

'Exactly. Wait a minute. What did you say? A new man? Spill.'

I replay riding into Callum's drive on the mobility scooter in my head and inwardly grimace.

'How did you meet him?' comes the next inevitable question.

, I'm ahead of her. 'It just happened,' I reply.

'So do I get to meet this new Callum?' asks Daisy.

'You do. Are you still staying at Sarah's at the moment?'

Daisy nods in confirmation.

'Good, stay there. Dougie will be fuming with me and he'll take it out on you if he can. You could come and stay at Callum's for a while, until you move to London? It would be safer?'

'Yes, possibly. Won't he mind?'

'Well, you should probably meet him first and see if you get on?'

Daisy smiles with excitement. I explain that Callum met Dougie and instantly knew he was an idiot. I am also concerned Dougie might go after Luke.

My ex must be fuming about his house. Even without proof, he'll suspect me.

'Will you find your brother for me, too?' I ask her.

She agrees, but wants to know if I'm really OK.

I assure her, 'I'm fighting fit.'

And I am. But I know the thoughts I am having now are dangerous.

***

Saturday 19th May
3.50 p.m.

A little later on my daily reconnaissance of the High Street, I pass the butcher's. Buying bones for the dogs, my mind turns to how to get rid of a body. I watch how the butcher fillets steak and what sort of knife he uses.

Next stop, the hardware shop. I gather a selection of knives, then realise this looks a bit suspicious. I want to wipe the handles I have tried, but decline for the same reason and the realisation that there will be security cameras, although I don't look up.

Once at school, we were taken on a careers trip to the abattoir... yes, really! I was already vegetarian, so would have refused to go, had I been listening when they announced the educational visit. I was staring at Philip Farmer's neck at the time. No one would have blamed me, it was the best seat in the class, my chair behind the blond bombshell.

However, I remember not the neck, but the white tiled death pit of the slaughterhouse. The stench of warm flesh, the last deep despairing breath of terror, the spring-loaded knife, the Pollock-esque splatterings of blood, thrown against the walls and ceilings, running down into a crimson pool at our feet. I thank God, to this day, that I didn't have to look into the cow's eyes. I didn't faint, though, and I never did a biology lesson again, or spoke to the teacher.

So today, I am set in my resolve; to find a way to kill and get away with the crime.

I hack away. Eventually I have a wide range of sizes of meat, some with bone, some without, so as to make the exercise a fair test. Around me, a scene of carnage. I change my plastic gloves, putting them into a box, so I can burn them later, and check I have my phone. I have put the meat samples into two plastic bags.

I travel in my car to the place where I found the pups. The field near the lay-by is free of birds, save a pheasant who looks like he has lost his way. I put some meat on the floor in the middle of the field and wait. The pheasant looks disturbed and flies over the hedge into the next field. The field is still covered in wheat stubble, the stalks left.

I wait for an hour, and realise that I need to disguise my presence with branches.

At dusk I feel it is time to go and come back tomorrow without any perfume on.

As I am walking towards my car, a crow squawks and lands near the meat feast. Looking sideways as they do, he takes a quick stab at the food and jumps away.

A seagull overhead calls out and also lands. I make myself tiny at the edge of the field and watch. These are smaller than the birds I expected to come, but probably noisier.

Other crows circle overhead and start to argue in the air. That is until, finally, a huge red kite soars into view and the other birds move away. The kite is superbly elegant, fully in control as she watches the scene. Adeptly she swoops and stands next to a large chunk of flesh, turning her head to eye the opposition. They cautiously take a grab when they can, until she jumps on one crow with her talons.

With this, other birds of prey appear. They circle the field and descend, causing a feeding frenzy. Soon all but the bones are gone.

I watch, mesmerised, thinking about how to get rid of the leftover calcium. Could the puppies get rid of the evidence?

I wait until only the crows remain and chase them off. Picking up the remains of gristle and bone, I return them to the carrier bags. Wow. I walk back to my car subdued and yet exhilarated. Here is a solution to my plan.

A CERTAIN KIND OF WONDERFUL

Several happy days pass whilst Callum and I get to know each other. I thank God several times a day for the change in my fortunes. However, I hide from *him* when my thoughts turn to how to quieten this incessant nagging in my soul. If only I wasn't so thorough, determined and perhaps pedantic?

SHOOTOUT AT THE HOLE IN THE FENCE
TWO WEEKS LATER
FRIDAY 2ND JUNE
5.05 p.m.

After days of searching the local library for an address, fate steps in. My chance, to level the scores.

I am in the High Street, sitting on a bench. The cashier from East Main Bank walks by and I give her my best sinister smile.

A mobility scooter sweeps past and I dart down, to hide my face. The man driving the machine looks at me as though I've lost my senses.

As I raise my head and gain my composure, I see Amy Grice coming out of a block of offices. Once I have set my resolve, I wonder what she's told them to get another job? She is quite a distance away and I set off to narrow the gap between us. She disappears inside the supermarket. I busy myself looking at adverts in the travel shop window nearby, until she reappears with a small carrier of shopping.

At the top of the street, she turns left and disappears from view. Has she seen me? I just manage to get to the corner, before she slips through the railings of some wasteland, and moves out of sight. I run to the fencing and search frantically for the gap.

Finding it, I run up the hill and can see her making her way along the uneven path. From the height of the rail bank, I see another track, which is shorter and intercepts her route. I run through the longer grass, without the grace of a gazelle, but with the determination of a wild cat, hunting its prey, until I am in a position to access her route. Slowing down, I walk casually towards Amy, who has her head down looking at her phone. Sweet.

She is as pleasant as expected, when I bar her way.

'What the fuck do you think you're doing?'

'Putting my mind at rest before I die,' I explain.

Amy looks very uncomfortable and starts to access the numbers on her phone.

'So you do recognise me?' I smirk as I knock the phone out of her hand and pick it up.

Even now she is obnoxious.

'You're alive, aren't you?'

'Have some manners,' I demand. 'Have you any idea the pain you have caused to all those people? Why?'

She's not going to have any idea, is she? She has to be lacking in intelligence to behave in such a way from the start.

Instead, she launches for my hair, throwing her full weight behind her and shrieking like a banshee. Keeping calm, I knock her, face down to the floor and swiftly tie her hands behind her back with my scarf. It is relatively easy. Probably because I've played it over in my mind so many times. She struggles to raise her face out of the dirt and continues to spit out venom.

'Get real, bitch,' she hisses.

I am trying hard to control my breathing. I have never restrained someone before. Never actually had a fight. I sit on her, until she stops struggling, then calmly say, 'I'm heavier than you.'

This annoys her, I am pleased to say.

'Fat bitch,' she proclaims. The kitchen of carnage, flashes across my mind. I realise I don't have a knife with me.

I laugh at her comments and partly because her face is turning crimson. Probably because I am a lot heavier than her?

'Yes, a fat and armed bitch,' I agree as I take a pair of scissors from my bag. 'So,' I muse, 'let's see how bald you will be, before you learn some manners.

Amy feigns boredom, but I can see in her eyes, as she attempts to peer behind her, that she doesn't want to lose her hair. At least she is appreciating to some degree how I felt when I heard my tragic news.

I return to the task. 'I'll ask you one more time, why?'

'Why not? Life is boring sometimes.'

I sit on my hands to stop myself from hitting the back of her head. She deserves it, but I may not be able to stop. I change tack. 'Do you know what a red kite is, Amy?'

'Der,' she insolently replies.

'*Milvus milvus*, British bird of prey. They eat anything, including dead rotting flesh. They usually hunt in pairs and like their own territory. But if you were to throw out a large juicy piece of meat, those scavenging birds of prey would make it disappear in less than a minute. Leaving no trace. You could easily make a body disappear that way.

'Anyway, who would bother looking for me? I'm already dead.'

Amy does not respond but avoids eye contact. I continue in a monotonous expressionless voice. Just like Mr. French at school, it wears you down in the end. I had forgotten that. Maybe now I'm onto something.

'Do you have a family?' I ask. I don't wait for an answer.

I stand to give my legs a rest.

'Well, you see I've been doing my homework. I know your parents find you a huge disappointment. Is that why they've disowned you?'

Amy struggles to turn her head and body, so she is half on her back, then flashes a defiant look at me. I turn her onto her back and sit on her legs.

'What is it?' I ask, 'Do you need to feel you have some power?'

Amy looks arrogantly straight at me and tries to rise. I push her down.

'Ah. But you have none. Soon you'll be in prison and those nasty big girls will make your life very difficult.'

'Yeah right,' she snarls. Even now she is fighting back. I'm not sure if I hate her, feel sorry for her or admire her grit.

I continue in the monotone voice. 'You just can't help yourself, can you. Are you ill? Something is eating you up inside? I'm actually really happy, thanks to a little help from you.'

I laugh. She doesn't like that.

'Isn't fate funny sometimes? I am enjoying an enormous feeling of satisfaction. I might even let you off today. Even with your abject lack of grace and your uncontrollable spite. I'll come back for you later though. When I feel bored.'

I pick up the scissors to put them in my bag.

Amy smirks.

I continue to lecture her. 'Luckily, I made the right decisions. I stand here today, satisfied and so, so pleased with my life. However, for my own mental health, I just need to take a small token.'

I reach forward and snip a large lock of hair from the front of Amy's head.

She struggles, but the deed is done.

'This is to remind you of what will happen, when you have the need to hurt someone, for the thrill.'

I put the scissors and the hair into my bag, but then return and take another chunk of hair from the top of her head. I confess, it gives me pleasure. I return the scissors once more into my bag. The drugs from the Savannah Club fall onto the floor.

Amy grins.

'I brought them for you,' I explain. 'To loosen your tongue, if I needed to. But I think you know nothing.' (I can't believe I haven't thought of this sooner.) 'However, I might let you try a few. They knocked a girl out for good, in the Savannah Club last week.'

Her face changes, her fear gives me credibility and I realise, I actually do have the power to end her life… with very little mess and probably, without incrimination. She knows it too.

In this moment, I find myself again. The beautiful, rational, lucid me. I have never taken drugs and only got them as a last resort, in case I couldn't deal with a slow, painful death. I smile with the realisation that the nightmare has now passed.

I laugh at Amy.

'I actually feel sorry for you. You have no morals and I don't believe in killing. Not my place.'

'Aren't you the high and mighty?' she retorts, still full of venom.

Bending down so my face is next to hers, I whisper politely, 'Yes. I am.'

'Not high and mighty enough to keep Dougie though.'

I erupt with laughter at the irony, that once again he has raised his ugly head and that I have, unequivocally, 'left the building'.

In my mind I can see Callum's face smiling at me and know instantly how much I have to lose.

I can't stop laughing with the realisation and relief.

'Dougie Stevens?' I howl. 'My God, even you wouldn't be that desperate, would you? Well, good luck with that, it'll be short, not sweet and you'll need to visit the health clinic afterwards.'

Amy looks ashamed, for a brief moment, but this is enough for me to feel gratified.

I stand, leaving her lying on her back on the ground, still tied, so I can walk across the wasteland, back to the street.

Amy struggles to free herself and to get onto her feet. I watch her momentarily before I set off. It is hard to decide if she looks like Houdini the escape artist or a hatchling crocodile. She snarls and with her hands still tied behind her back, she runs after me.

I am walking casually across the wasteland. I can hear Amy shouting behind me, but I do not turn. There's no point. I've had my say and she is as unfeeling and selfish, as a dull gritstone.

'Wait, you stupid bitch,' she screams. At least I have made her sound deranged.

'Hey bitch, think you're Queen Bee now?'

I turn around and walk back to her, wrestling her to the floor and rubbing her face in the dirt.

'Yes,' I reply, leaving her lying in the dust.

I continue to walk and come to the place where local people illegally cross the rail track as a short cut to the shopping precinct. I look both ways, to check if it is safe to proceed. I arrive on the other side, seconds later. I can hear her advancing again, behind me. She must have struggled to her feet. With the anger of a petulant child, she screams at the top of her voice, 'You won't get rid of me now. You should have stayed hidden.'

I keep walking. 'Whatever,' I say quietly to myself.

'I'm gonna follow you. Find your weak spot,' she shouts.

I am near the other side fence now. I keep walking. Has she freed her hands, I wonder?

I can hear her footsteps stomping behind me, getting faster as she shouts, losing her breath through her anger.

'Run off then, stupid bitch,' she rasps.

A much shriller sound suddenly demands the attention of the evening air. This gives way to a thunderous, heavy thudding of metal on metal. A train sweeps past at high speed. I turn as the carriages flash by, at neck-breaking speed. The rhythm sounds its drum roll along the heated tracks. The high-speed motion suspends time, as I watch. Has it taken her with it?

When the train has passed, the look on her face as she re-appears on the other side of the track, makes it worth all my efforts. Such sweet serendipity. The serene silence in the wake of the train and Amy's look of horror, gives me living proof that she now understands, what it feels like, to be that close to death. Her skin ashen, her eyes wide, her face contorted like the ghost of Jacob Marley. Too shocked to turn her face from mine, she observes the wide and delighted fullness of my smile, before she drops to the ground.

I ensure I maintain the eye contact, then turn and walk swiftly away. When I turn back, she is still crouching on the ground and sobbing.

'Now we're even, madam,' I say to myself. I put my hands together in thanks.

All nuts crack eventually. You just need to find the right tool.

SWEET AS A NUT
FRIDAY 2ND JUNE
7.15 p.m.

CALLUM is working on his computer when I walk in. I soak in the glory of his profile and his kind mouth, until it starts to feel wrong. He is excited about his reading material.

'Look at this. That doctors' surgery you used to go to has been prosecuted for altering the diagnoses of dozens of patients. They think one woman was responsible. She's gone missing. The firm have been suspended because of the sheer number of lawsuits filed against them,' he genuinely enthuses.

'Yes, I heard about it.' I try and sound objective, not because I want to conceal what's happened: I just want a clean start.

He wants to know if I think this is what happened to me.

I agree it could be, but we won't know until they analyse my notes.

'Apparently the press had an anonymous tip off,' he reports.

I don't think he is trying to trick me. I hope I am sounding analytical and uninvolved. It is still worthwhile changing the subject, though.

'Shall we take the dogs out for a run in the fields? I love the feeling of the sun on my back,' I suggest. This is indeed true. I am still feeling the joy of life to the full. Including, the way he holds my hand as we stroll along. I decide to continue to push my luck.

'Then maybe you could meet Daisy?' I offer.

'Sure,' he replies, in his usual laidback way. I try not to sigh too loudly with the contentment, in case some maker of the universe realises I am happy and casts another thunderbolt.

I make sure Callum knows how grateful I am though.

'Thank you.' I beam up at him. 'I want to make sure my children are safe. Thinking I was losing them has made me miss them even more. It won't be for long. They've already flown the nest once.'

'I just want them near me for a while longer. I know they've got their own lives. I knew that when they left for university, they probably wouldn't come back...OK it's about my security, I admit it.'

'We can ask them though?'

'It will be good having the house full of life again,' he tells me. He picks up two glasses of wine, and hands me one.

'I'll drink to that,' I announce.

'Here's to the fantastically fruitful finger of fate.' He raises his glass and we clink before sipping.

I nod and hug him. The dogs lift their heads, but leave us to our show of affection.

'I do appreciate what you've done for me, you know,' I tell him.

He cheekily replies that it is kinda good for him too.

This inspires me to hug him again.

'Well yes that,' I say, 'But so much more. How you've had my back. With me running around like a maniac, it might have felt like I didn't notice your kindness… but I did.'

I kiss him. So that he knows how much I appreciate his sweetness and support.

'I've watched you and your determination,' he says. 'It was entertaining, enlightening… and intriguing. It was easy to wait.'

I try to gather some context, so that I might sustain this euphoria I feel.

'In all the great love stories, Romeo and Juliette, Helen of Troy… and sweet, sweet Tess, there is always a tragic ending. I expected the same,' I explain.

He laughs heartily.

'You think you haven't had enough tragedy?' he asks.

'Well yes, but when I think about how many times things could have gone even more wrong. They still could. You know you saved me, don't you?'

Callum laughs and strokes my hair.

'Helping you has made me feel hopeful and a little more in control,' he explains.

'Good. There's no way I could ever have dreamed it would end like this. Do you think there's any chance it will last?' I chance my luck by asking.

Callum contemplates his answer. 'A happy ending? I suppose we won't know for sure, until we look back in sixty years' time and remember how we started.' I stare at him, then turn and sink into his arms.

The dogs stare up from their baskets, but then return to their own dreams.

Later in the bathroom mirror I ask myself, *Who would have thought I could be this happy?*

I guess the message is, take no prisoners, use what you've got and never give up hope.

Oh, and believe in the karma of the universe. You never know what it might bring you.